"Will you marry me, Beatrice?

"Oh, not immediately," Gijs went on smoothly. "You will need time to get used to the idea."

"Why on earth do you want to marry me?" she asked in a sudden rush. "We don't even know each other well. Besides, I don't..."

"You seek romance? Naturally, I suppose all women do. But where has it got you? I won't pretend lifelong devotion, only a sincere liking, an abiding friendship and a promise to care for your happiness."

"But you don't..." she began, and he finished for her.

"Love you? Neither of us has had much success with love, have we?"

Betty Neels spent her childhood and youth in Devon, England before training as a nurse and midwife. She was an army nursing sister during the war, married a Dutchman and subsequently lived in Holland for fourteen years. She lives with her husband in Dorset, and has a daughter and a grandson. Her hobbies are reading, animals, old buildings and writing. Betty started to write on retirement from nursing, incited by a lady in a library bemoaning the lack of romance novels.

WEDDING BELLS FOR BEATRICE
Betty Neels

Harlequin Books

TORONTO • NEW YORK • LONDON
AMSTERDAM • PARIS • SYDNEY • HAMBURG
STOCKHOLM • ATHENS • TOKYO • MILAN
MADRID • WARSAW • BUDAPEST • AUCKLAND

ISBN 0-373-15617-0

WEDDING BELLS FOR BEATRICE

First North American Publication 1995.

CHAPTER ONE

LADY DOWLEY'S Christmas party was in full swing, an event which achieved the very pinnacle of social life in the village of Little Estling, remotely situated as it was some nine miles from Aylesbury and well away from the main road. Remote though it was, it had more than its fair share of landed gentry and the retired professional classes scattered in and around the small place, carrying on tradition: cricket in summer, garden parties, church bazaars, carol-singing at Christmas...

The large ornate drawing-room in Lady Dowley's Victorian mansion was full of people, not because she was especially liked in the neighbourhood but because she offered refreshments of a kind most of them were quite unable to afford: smoked salmon, Parma ham, delicious bits and pieces poised on minuscule scraps of toast. The wines were good too; her late husband had assembled a nice cellar before he died. She was an overbearing woman, still handsome in a middle-aged way and prone to interfere in other people's affairs and with a deep-rooted conviction that she was always right. It would have upset her very much to know that her friends and acquaintances pitied her and, despite not liking her over-much, would be prepared to go to her aid if it should ever be required.

Happily unaware of this, she surged to and fro, being gracious to those she considered a little beneath her socially and effusive to those she saw as her equals, and presently she fetched up before a middle-aged, thick-set man with a calm wise face and shrewd eyes.

'Dr Crawley, how delightful to see you.' She glanced around her. 'And your dear wife?' She didn't give him time to answer. 'And your lovely daughter?'

Dr Crawley said comfortably, 'They are here, Lady Dowley, no doubt having a good gossip with someone or other. You're keeping well? And Phoebe?'

'I told her that she simply had to come—I go to all the trouble of asking any number of interesting people.' She looked over his shoulder. 'You must excuse me; there is a very old firm friend—do remember me to your wife if I shouldn't see her ... Perhaps she will come to tea soon.'

Dr Crawley made a non-committal noise. His wife, a sweet-tempered woman with a retiring disposition, was none the less the granddaughter of an earl, therefore to be cultivated by his hostess. Dr Crawley, whose family had lived on the outskirts of the village for generations, and who knew every single inhabitant, gave a derisive snort and then turned to see who was tapping him on the shoulder.

His daughter Beatrice was a head taller than he, a splendidly shaped girl standing five feet ten inches tall in her bare feet and as pretty as a picture. She had light brown hair, long and straight and coiled in the nape of her neck, large grey eyes with sweeping lashes the same colour as her hair, a delicate nose and a wide, sweetly curved mouth above a determined chin. She was smiling.

'Father, cheer up—we'll be able to leave in another half-hour or so. I've left Mother with Mrs Hodge discussing knitting patterns.' She stopped abruptly as a pair of hands covered her eyes from behind. 'Derek, it is you, isn't it? Has the path. lab thrown you out at last?'

She put up a hand to her forehead. 'Don't you dare to make my hair untidy, it took me hours...!'

The hands dropped and she was turned round, smiling, offering a cheek for his casual kiss, aware that there was someone with him. A man of vast proportions with grey hair cut very short and heavy-lidded blue eyes. It was an unpleasant shock to see that he was looking at her with a detached coolness so that her smile faded. He doesn't like me, she thought uncertainly, but we don't even know each other...

'Beatrice, this is Gijs van der Eekerk—Gijs, this is Beatrice Crawley; we've known each other since we were trundled out in our prams. Years ago.'

She shot him a look—any minute now he would tell this man how old she was. She held out a hand and said, 'How do you do?' and had it engulfed in a firm grip. 'Are you visiting Derek?' she asked, wanting to hear his voice.

'For a day or so.' He stood, looking down at her, making no effort to hold the kind of social conversation she expected.

'You're Dutch?' she asked for the sake of something to say. 'You know England well?'

'I come over fairly frequently—this is a very pretty part of the country.'

She agreed and wished heartily that Derek and her father would stop whatever they were saying to each other and help out with the talk.

'What a pity it is that convention prevents us from saying what we wish to say and forces us to make small talk about the weather.'

He had a deep voice and his English was faultless with only a slight accent. She stared at him, at a loss for words for a moment. Then she said, 'That wouldn't do at all.' She spoke sharply. 'But I think you would like to.'

He smiled then, a small smile which made her feel foolish although she had no idea why. 'Indeed I would, and I must warn you that at times I do.' He paused. 'Speak my mind.'

'Then I am sorry for whoever has to listen to you,' she said with a snap. 'You'll excuse me? I see someone I want to talk to.'

She left him and he watched her go before joining her father and his friend.

She knew everyone there, going from group to group, exchanging gossip, and all the while knowing that she would have to find the wretched man and apologise for her rudeness. All the same, she reminded herself, she had meant it.

Her mother and father were on the point of leaving when she saw him again, talking to the Reverend Mr Perkins. She made her way slowly towards them, intent on getting the business over since they weren't likely to meet again.

The rector saw her first. 'Beatrice—I've been wanting a word with you—come over to the rectory in the morning, will you...?' He looked apologetically at the man beside him. 'Christmas, you know—such a busy time.' He held out a hand. 'A pleasure meeting you, and I hope it may be repeated.' He beamed at Beatrice. 'I leave you in good hands; Beatrice is a sweet girl.' He trotted off, unaware of the effect of his words.

Her companion lifted his eyebrows. 'I'm delighted to hear that,' he said pleasantly, 'and, I must admit, surprised.'

Beatrice's magnificent bosom swelled with sudden temper. 'I might have known,' she said bitterly. 'I came to apologise for being rude, but I'm not going to now.'

He said to infuriate her still more, 'No, no, why should you? You have a very good expression in English—to vent one's spleen—so very apt, I have always thought. Besides, bad temper suits you. Pray don't give a thought to apologising.'

'Well, I won't. It is a very good thing that we are never likely to see each other again, for we don't get on.'

'Apparently not.' He sounded uninterested, waiting for her to end the conversation.

'Goodbye,' said Beatrice. If she had known how to flounce she would have done so, but she didn't, so she walked away with her chin up and a very straight back. She looked just as delightful from the back, the man reflected, watching her go.

Beatrice, sitting beside her father as he drove home through the scattering of houses and up the hill on the other side to where they lived, replied rather absentmindedly to her mother's comments about the party, while she reflected, very much to her surprise, that she wished that she could meet Gijs van der Eekerk again. Not because she liked him, she hastened to assure herself, but to find out more about him.

Her mother's voice interrupted her thoughts. 'Will you see Tom tomorrow?'

'Tom?' Beatrice sounded vague, 'Oh, I don't know...'

Mrs Crawley's maternal instincts were at once on the alert. 'What a charming man that was who came with Derek—I wonder where he comes from and what he does...?'

Beatrice muttered, 'I've no idea,' and her father made no effort to enlighten them; instead he made some placid remark about the evening.

Christmas was only two days away. George, the Crawleys' son, a medical student nine years younger than his sister, would be coming home for two days' leave and two elderly aunts would be arriving in the morning to spend Christmas—there was more than enough to keep Beatrice busy what with helping her mother prepare for Christmas and helping with the flowers at the church. Making mince pies and arranging holly wreaths made a welcome change from her job at St Justin's Hospital in the heart of the East End of London. She liked her work—being responsible for the smooth running and maintainance of the extensive laboratory attached to the hospital. She had gone there straight from her domestic science course and gradually worked her way up to her present job—as high as she could go. Sometimes the thought that she would be there for ever crept into her mind—twenty-eight was no longer the first flush of youth and despite several offers of marriage she had felt no urge to accept any of them. There was always Tom, of course, who tended to behave as though he had only to beckon and she would come. He was ambitious, working his way ruthlessly to a consultant's status, and she sometimes suspected that the love he professed for her was a good deal less than his anticipation of a path smoothed for him by a father-in-law who knew all the right people. He was a pleasant companion and she saw a good deal of him— had even invited him home for a weekend. Her mother and father had been hospitable and friendly but she was aware that they hadn't liked him.

George arrived soon after breakfast on Christmas Eve, laden with a bag of washing, a crate of beer and a great many parcels. 'Presents,' he explained cheerfully, 'but I've not had time to wrap them up—I know you'll do it for me, Beatrice.'

'I'll be sorry for your wife when you get one,' said Beatrice good-naturedly and filled the washing-machine before going in search of paper and labels. He sat at the kitchen table drinking mugs of coffee and telling her what to write on the labels in between answering his mother's questions about his work. He was just starting his second year and had passed his first exams; he loved it, he assured her, and Beatrice, who had a very good idea of a medical student's life, smiled at him. They got on well together despite the difference in their ages and, perhaps because of this, he had always confided in her.

She finished the presents, cut him a hunk of the big fruitcake on the dresser and went to answer the doorbell.

It was the aunts, elderly and rather old-fashioned, having been driven from Aylesbury in a hired car. They were sitting in the back, very erect, their faces composed under formidable felt hats. Beatrice greeted them and the chauffeur, asked him to bring in the luggage and went to help her aunts out of the car. They were both quite capable of helping themselves but it never entered their heads to do so. They never spoke of the lordly head of the family but they didn't forget him either. Certain standards had to be maintained; they reminded each other of this from time to time and they had no intention of altering a way of life which had been normal in their youth, but despite their stiff manners they were dear old things—Beatrice loved them.

She eased them out carefully, kissed the proffered cheeks and led the way indoors.

Later that morning, the old ladies settled in and the chores done, Beatrice got into the elderly cloak hanging behind the kitchen door and worn by everyone in the family and took herself off to the church to find Mr Perkins.

He was putting a plug on the fairy-lights on the Christmas tree and making a bad job of it. Beatrice took it from him, rearranged the wires, screwed them down and handed it back to him. He was a nice old man, everyone in the village liked him, but he needed a great deal of looking after since his wife had died.

He thanked her warmly. 'I asked you to come and see me but I'm afraid I can't remember why.' And before she could suggest anything, he said, 'What a very nice man that was with young Derek—I wish I had had more time to talk to him. I trust we shall see him again...'

'Well, I shouldn't think so,' said Beatrice. 'He's Dutch, you know, and only here on a visit.'

'A pity. Ah, I've remembered what I wished to ask you, my dear. If you could give a hand with the children during the blessing of the crib?'

'Yes, of course. Six o'clock this evening, isn't it?'

'So kind. When do you go back to your work, Beatrice?'

'Boxing Day, in the evening. It's lovely to be home for Christmas. I must fly—the aunts and George are staying with us, and Mother needs a hand in the kitchen.'

'Yes, yes, of course.' He smiled gently. 'Run along... It seems only the other day that you were a little girl. How old are you now, Beatrice?'

'Twenty-eight.'

'You should be married with children.'

'As soon as I can find a husband I'll do just that, and you shall marry us.' She laughed as she spoke, but really, she reflected as she sped home, it was no laughing matter. She hadn't lacked for prospective husbands but somehow none of them had touched her heart. 'I dare say I shall make a splendid aunt,' she said to Horace, the elderly cat who had invited himself to live with them some years ago and had been there ever since.

Horace jumped down off the wall and followed her into the house. He had long ago realised that when she was at home he could be sure of getting his meals on time. Her romantic future was of no concern to him.

She hadn't been home for Christmas for three years and she enjoyed every moment of it, especially the blessing of the crib with the children milling around, some of them dressed in curtains and their mothers' dressing-gowns and gold paper crowns, enacting their own little play round the crib. Beatrice, nipping smartly to and fro, shushing the noisiest of them and rearranging the curtains which had come adrift, thoroughly enjoyed herself. She went home to supper when it was all over and listened to her aunts' gentle reminiscences of their youth and presently slipped out of the room to join George and listen to his account of his life at the hospital. She gathered that it wasn't bad—he was clever and when he chose worked hard and didn't mind the long hours of study. He had friends too, and his social life, as far as she could gather, was a lively one.

'What about you?' he wanted to know. 'Isn't it about time you got married?' He added, 'What about Tom?'

She took this in good part. 'It's a funny thing, George, I've done my best to fall in love with him, but it's no good. You see, I don't think it's me he wants, it's a quick way to the top, and Daddy could help him...'

'Toss him out, my dear. Isn't there anyone else?' She said no in a doubtful voice while Gijs van der Eekerk's handsome features floated around in her head. She shook it vigorously and said 'no' again quite violently. Why should she think of him when she so disliked him?

George gave her a curious look and said nothing. So there was someone, even if she didn't know it herself. The thought pleased him; he had never liked Tom, who patronised him.

Christmas Day, its traditions never varying from year to year, came and went with its presents, church in the morning, turkey and Christmas pudding, crackers and cake, and then Boxing Day, pleasantly easygoing after the hustle and bustle, followed it all too swiftly. Beatrice loaded her bag into her own Mini, added a box of food which her mother considered necessary to augment what she considered to be the hospital stodge, hugged everyone and promised to be home again as soon as she could get a couple of days off, and drove away, down the lane past Lady Dowley's imposing house and through the village. A pity Derek had a week's leave, she reflected; she saw very little of him at the hospital but from time to time they saw each other going their various ways and very occasionally they had gone out to supper when they were both free.

She took a side-road to Aylesbury and presently joined the A41 which took her to the outskirts of London. She was a good driver and there was very little traffic. She went across the city, a lengthy business, weaving in and out of streets becoming more and more shabby as she went east. Presently she could see the bulk of St Justin's ahead of her, towering over the rows of grimy little houses and shops, and turned in through its open gateway to park her car at the back of the hospital and go in through a side-door. It opened on to a passage going left and right and she took the one going away from the hospital to the newer block which housed the path. lab and the various departments appertaining to it. Her flatlet was on the top floor, a large room, nicely furnished, with its own little shower-room and tiny kitchenette. The view from its windows was depressing enough—chimney-pots and boarded-up shops and warehouses—but she kept an array of pot plants on the sills which screened the worst of them and had added over the years bright cushions, and pretty lamps so that the place was welcoming. She was a lucky young woman, she told herself as she unpacked her bag. She had a good job, reasonably well paid, and she liked her work. On the ground floor she had her office where she dealt with the cleaners, the part-time cook who came in from time to time to provide the laboratory staff with meals if they weren't able to go to the hospital canteen, and, as well as this, she paid the bills, and worked her way through a great deal of paperwork which the hospital administration demanded of her. She kept a motherly eye on everyone too, reporting sickness or injuries, and she dealt with the mundane running of the place—the plumber, painters, maintenance men—and, over and above that, dealt with the foibles of the varied learned gentlemen who worked there with their assistants. She was known rather grandly as the administrator but she thought of herself as the housekeeper.

She was opening a can of soup when the telephone rang. 'You're back,' said Tom. 'I thought of you living in the lap of luxury while the rest of us worked ourselves into the ground. I suppose you went to several marvellous parties...'

'One,' said Beatrice and wondered why she felt no sympathy for him.

'Lucky girl. How about telling me all about it tomorrow evening? I shall be free for a few hours—we might go and have a meal somewhere. Seven o'clock suit you?'

She frowned, faintly annoyed that he was so sure of her accepting. 'I shall be busy tomorrow—everyone will be working late; there's the seminar on the following day...'

'For heaven's sake!' He sounded as peevish as a spoilt child. 'Why must you fuss over those old back-room boys?'

'I'm not fussing, just doing my job.' She spoke sharply and he was quick to hear it.

'Sorry, Beatrice—I'm tired, I suppose. Let's meet around eight o'clock and have a cup of coffee—tell you what, I'll be in the car and if you aren't there by half-past I'll know you couldn't make it.'

She couldn't in all fairness object to that; she agreed and hung up with the nagging thought that perhaps she had been unreasonable. He was a busy man and good at his job and she was aware that sooner or later he would ask her to marry him, and always at the back of her head was the unpleasant thought that he didn't love her—not with the kind of love she wanted, anyway. She was sure that if she had been a hospital clerk with a father who had no influential friends he would never have entertained the idea of marrying her. On the other hand, he was ambitious and hard-working and had a charming manner when he needed it; he would make a success of his career and she would have a pleasant enough life. She wandered around the room, picking things up and putting them down again, feeling unsettled.

There was plenty to keep her occupied the next day. Very neat in her dark grey dress with its white collar and cuffs, she toured the whole place, making sure that the domestic staff were doing what they were supposed to do, calculating with the cook just how many morning coffees and afternoon teas she would have to get ready. She hadn't had the list of names yet, which was vexing, although she did know the number of men who would be attending; at least she could make sure that the lecture-room near her small office could be got ready.

The various laboratories were all hard at work again after Christmas and she was kept busy: an urgent call for a new light bulb, a worn washer on one of the sink taps, demands for hot milk from Professor Moore, the dermatologist, who had a frightful cold, more demands for Panadol from his secretary, who was convinced that she had caught it.

Really, thought Beatrice, I'm actually the caretaker with a bit of book-keeping thrown in. Administrator was far too grand a word for it.

Several of the labs were working late; she sent up coffee and sandwiches to the technicians and took herself off to her flat. It was already after seven o'clock and she would have liked to have a shower, get into her dressing-gown and eat her supper by the small gas fire, with a good book. Instead she showered and changed into a green wool dress and put on a thick wool coat, rammed a woolly cap on to her head, found gloves and handbag and went out of the building, along the passage and through the hospital until she reached the entrance. Tom was there; she could see him sitting in his car, reading the paper. He saw her too as she crossed the fore-court, folded the paper and opened the door for her.

'I was going to give you another five minutes, but I guessed you would come.' He sounded smug.

His tone implied that she would always come running... never mind if she were tired or cross or just not feeling like going out. She busied herself with her safety-belt and stayed silent. He made it worse by remarking that she would feel better after a drink and launching into a very complicated account of his own busy day.

Beatrice, feeling ruffled because he hadn't bothered to ask her if she had had a good Christmas, wished she hadn't come. And why had she come? she asked herself. Force of habit? She had allowed herself to drift into something more than casual friendship with Tom and it struck her now that it was time it ended. She was a kind-hearted girl and although he was exasperating her now she was honest enough to admit that she had enjoyed several pleasant evenings with him when they had first become friendly; it was only later that she'd realised that he was using her as a means to an end. Perhaps she could talk to him presently.

'We'll go to the Tower Thistle,' he told her, 'have something in the bar. I mustn't be away for more than an hour or so, and I'll probably get called up during the night. I could do with some sleep too. We had a splendid party on Christmas night, didn't get to bed until two o'clock and got called out just after five. Ah, well, it isn't for ever—once I get a decent private practice—a partnership, perhaps...' He went on at some length, sure of himself and her attention.

She was only half listening; the first of the specialists would be arriving in time for coffee in the morning and she was going over her careful catering once more, saying, 'Oh yes?' and, 'Really?' and, 'Of course,' at intervals. Once at the hotel, a vast place which she didn't much like, she had to give Tom her un-

divided attention, sitting opposite him at a
table in the bar, eating sandwiches and
drinking a glass of white wine. The sandwiches were small and elegant, garnished with
cress, and Beatrice, who was hungry, could
have eaten the lot.

'You'll have had a good square meal,' said
Tom comfortably, 'but do devour one—
there's just enough horseradish with the beef.'

She nibbled one, thinking of fried eggs on
baked beans and a huge pot of tea or coffee.
It was a funny thing, but Tom wasn't the kind
of man you could ask to take you to the
nearest McDonald's. If he wasn't hungry, then
you weren't either, or, for that matter, if he
assumed that you weren't hungry and he was
he wouldn't ask you if you were...

It was very noisy in the bar and he had to
raise his voice when he spoke. He put his
elbows on the table and leaned towards her.
'Isn't it time that we made a few plans?'

'Plans? What plans?'

He smiled at her indulgently. 'Our future—
I've another six months to do at St Justin's
then I'll be ready to get a practice—buy a
partnership. I'll need some financial backing
but your father could put me in touch with
all the right people—he may be a country GP
but he knows everyone worth knowing,

doesn't he? Besides, your mother...' He paused delicately and his smile widened and he added coaxingly, 'Once all that is settled we might get married.'

Beatrice sought for words; the only ones she could think of were very rude, so she kept silent. He must have been very sure of her—his proposal, if you could call it that, had been an afterthought. She twiddled the glass in her hand and wondered what would happen if she threw it at him. She said very quietly, 'But I don't want to marry you, Tom.'

He laughed, 'Don't be a silly girl, of course you do. Don't pretend that I've taken you by surprise. We've been going out together now for weeks and I've made no secret of the fact that I want to settle down once I'm away from St Justin's.'

'I don't remember you asking me if I had any plans for the future,' observed Beatrice. She was bubbling over with rage but she looked quite serene. 'But you—your plan was to get my father to put in a good word for you—I don't know where Mother comes in... Oh, of course—being the granddaughter of an earl.'

'A little name-dropping never does any harm,' answered Tom complacently. 'Can't you just see it in the *Telegraph*? "Beatrice,

daughter of Dr and the Hon. Mrs Crawley".'
He sat back in his chair, smiling at her.

'Tom, I have just told you—I don't want
to marry you. I'm sorry if you got the impression that I did. We've been good friends
and enjoyed each other's company but that's
all, isn't it?'

'I'm very fond of you, old girl.' He didn't
notice her wince. 'You'll be a splendid wife,
all the right connections and so on. I'll make
a name for myself in no time.'

The colossal conceit of him, reflected
Beatrice; it was like trying to dent a steel plate
with a teaspoon. He hadn't once said that he
loved her...

Characteristically, he didn't ask if she
wanted to go but finished his drink with an
air of satisfaction at a job well done and
asked, 'Ready? I've got a couple of cases that
I must look at.'

She got into the car beside him and he drove
back to the hospital in silence. At the entrance he said, 'We must get together again
as soon as possible—you'll have to give up
your job here, of course.'

'Tom,' she tried to sound reasonable, 'you
don't understand. I don't want to marry you
and I have no intention of giving up my job
here. I think it might be better if we don't see

each other again. Surely we can part friends?'
She added coldly, 'There must be plenty of
suitable girls from whom you can choose a
wife.'

'Oh, you are being a silly girl. You'll change
your mind, I'll see to that. I'll give you a ring
when I'm free.'

He sat in the car with the engine still
running, waiting for her to get out, and the
moment that she did he shot away with a
casual wave. Not the behaviour of a man who
had only half an hour ago proposed to her.
Bottled-up rage and hurt feelings choked her
as she crossed the courtyard. It was cold and
very dark once she was away from the brightly
lit entrance. The bulk of the new block behind
the hospital loomed ahead of her; there were
still a good many lights burning—several of
the path. labs were still working. She wished
with all her heart that she were at home, able
to go to her room and cry her eyes out without
anyone wanting to know why unless she
wished to tell them. Held-back tears filled her
eyes and dribbled down her cheeks; there was
no one to tell here . . .!

There was, however. Gijs van der Eekerk
reached the door at the same time as she did;
his large gloved hand covered hers as she put
it on the door-handle.

He took no notice of her stifled scream. 'They told me that you would be back—that you had gone out for an hour with Dr Ford. I thought we might bury the hatchet over supper.'

He took the hand off the door and turned her round so that the dim light above the door shone on her face.

His 'tut-tut' was uttered with all the mild good-natured concern of an uncle or elder brother. 'Tears? May I ask why?'

'Don't you tut-tut at me,' said Beatrice crossly, 'and if I want to cry I shall and I shan't tell you why.'

He offered a large handkerchief. 'No, no, of course you shan't and a good weep is very soothing to the nerves, only wouldn't it be better if you wept in a warmer spot?'

She blew her nose. 'Yes, of course if would. If you would let me go in I can get some peace and quiet in my flat.'

'Splendid.' He opened the door and, when she had gone through, followed her.

'I'm quite all right, thank you,' said Beatrice, belatedly remembering her manners. Then she added, 'How did you get here?'

'I'm to read a paper here in the morning.'

'You're a doctor—a surgeon . . . ?'

'A haematologist. Let us go to your flat. You can tidy yourself before we go somewhere and have supper.'

'I don't want...that is, thank you very much, but I don't want any supper and there is no need for you to come with me.'

'Ah—you had a meal with that young man who drove off in such a hurry?'

'You were spying?'

'No—no—I was just getting out of my car.' He sounded so reasonable that she felt guilty of her suspicions and muttered,

'Sorry.'

'So now let us do as I suggested, there's a good girl,' His avuncular manner was reassuring; she led the way to the top floor and opened the door of her flat.

He took her coat in the tiny hallway. 'Run along and do your face,' he advised her, and went round the room, turning on the lamps and closing the curtains and, despite the faint warmth from the central heating, he turned on the gas fire too. The sleeping area of the room was curtained off and she set to, repairing the damage done to her face and redoing her hair, listening to him strolling around the room, whistling softly. She reflected that he was the first man to be there; it had never entered her head to invite Tom or any of the young doctors who from time to time had asked her out, and she wondered now what on earth had possessed her to do so now. Not that she had invited him; he had come with her as though it were a perfectly natural thing to do. She frowned as she stuck pins into her coil of hair; he was altogether too much and she would tell him so—show him the door, politely, of course.

He was sitting, his coat off, in one of the small easy-chairs by the fire, but he got up as she crossed the room, watching her. 'That's better. Supposing that you tell me what upset you then if you want to cry again you can do so in warmth and comfort before we go to supper.'

'I have no intention of crying again, Doctor, nor do I want supper.'

Her insides rumbled as she said it, giving the lie to her words. She might have saved her breath.

He pulled forward a chair invitingly. 'Did he jilt you or did you jilt him?'

She found herself sitting opposite him. 'Well, neither really,' she began.

'A quarrel? It will help to talk about it and since I am a complete stranger to you too you can say what you like, I'll listen and forget about it.'

She was taking leave of her senses of course, confiding in this man.

'Well,' she began, 'it is all a bit of a muddle.'

CHAPTER TWO

THE professor was a splendid listener; Beatrice quite forgot that he was there once she had started. 'It's probably all my fault. Tom's attractive and amusing and I suppose I was flattered and it got a kind of habit to go out with him when he asked me. I didn't really notice how friendly we'd become. I took him home for a weekend...'

She paused. 'Mother and Father didn't like him very much—oh, they didn't say so, I just knew, and then lately he began to talk about buying a practice and making a name for himself, only he said he would need some backing and he began to talk about Father—he's a GP, and not well known or anything, but he does know a lot of important medical men, and Tom discovered that Mother was an earl's granddaughter.' She paused to say wildly, 'I don't know why I'm telling you all this...'

He said in a detached voice, 'As I have already said, we're more or less strangers, unlikely to be more than that. I'm just a face to talk to...go on!'

'I—I was getting doubtful, I mean I wasn't sure if I liked him as much as I thought I did, if you see what I mean, and then this evening he wanted me to go out with him; he was very persistent so I went. He took me to the Tower Thistle—it's a hotel, not too far away.' She heaved a great sigh. 'He ate all but one of the sandwiches—he said that no doubt I had had a good square meal. I knew that I didn't love him then—well, any girl would, wouldn't she?' She gave her companion a brief glance and found his face passive and impersonal. 'Then he said it was time we thought about our future, that he would need financial backing to get a partnership and that Father would be a great help. He even suggested that he could use Mother's name to give him a start; he actually described the notice of our engagement in the *Telegraph*. I told him that I didn't want to marry him—he hadn't actually asked me, just took me for granted—and then he just laughed.' She sniffed and added in a furious voice, 'I won't be taken for granted.'

'Certainly not,' agreed the professor. 'This—Tom—? seems to be a singularly thick-skinned man.' His voice was as avuncular as his manner. 'Do you see much of him during your working hours?'

'Hardly ever. I'm here all day and he works on the medical wards, but he telephones and I have to answer in case it's one of the profs, wanting hot milk or sandwiches.'

'Hot milk?' The professor looked taken aback.

'Well, some of them are getting on a bit and they forget to go to meals or go home when they're supposed to. I suppose professors are all the same, a bit absentminded...'

She gave him a startled look. 'You're a professor, you must be if you're coming to the seminar tomorrow.'

'Well, yes, I am, but I must assure you at once that I am unlikely to need hot milk. Which reminds me, we still have to have supper.'

'I don't want...' began Beatrice, saw the quizzical lift of his eyebrows and added quickly, 'Thank you, that would be nice—if it could be somewhere quiet? I'm not dressed for anywhere smart. Do you know London?'

'I find my way around,' admitted the professor modestly. 'Get your coat and let us see what we can find.'

When she came back ready to leave he had turned off the fire, left one lamp burning and had the door open. As they went down to the entrance the building was very quiet and, despite the heating, chilly. It was even colder outside and he took her arm and hurried her round to the corner of the forecourt where he had parked his car.

'You drove over?' asked Beatrice, silently admiring the understated luxury of the big Bentley as she was ushered into it.

He got in beside her and drove out of the forecourt with the minimum of fuss. 'I have several other hospitals to visit while I'm here. It saves time if I have the car.'

She sat quietly, realising almost at once that he knew London well, not hesitating at all until he stopped in Camden Passage, got out and opened her door, locked it, put money in the parking meter and led her across the pavement to the restaurant. She had heard of it—Frederick's—but she had never been there and she hung back a little, wondering if she was wearing the right clothes.

'Now don't start fussing,' begged the professor, just as though she had voiced her doubts. 'You're perfectly adequately dressed,' he added as a concession to her uncertainty. 'You look very nice.'

A remark her brother George might have made, and one hardly adequate; she dressed well, knowing what suited her and that she could afford to buy it—the tweed coat and woolly cap were suitable for a quick drink on a cold winter's night but not what she would have chosen for a late dinner in a restaurant.

She was propelled with gentle remorselessness through the entrance. 'You can leave your coat there,' said the professor, and bade the doorman good evening.

When she joined him, reassured by her reflection in the cloakroom's mirrors, he was talking to the *maître d'* who, as she reached them, led them to a table by a window, paused to recommend the pheasant, which he said was excellent, wished them an enjoyable meal and gave way to a waiter.

'You like pheasant?' asked the professor. 'Or perhaps you would prefer something else.'

She studied the menu and suddenly felt famished. 'I'd like the pheasant, please...'

'The lobster mousse is delicious—shall we start with that?'

She would have started with a hunk of bread, lunch having been a sketchy affair of soup and a roll and her solitary beef sandwich already long forgotten.

She ate the mousse with pleasure. It was amazing what good food did to restore one's good spirits; by the time they had disposed of the pheasant and she was deciding on a sweet she had quite recovered and was once more the level-headed supervisor, making polite conversation over the dinner-table. All the same during a pause in the talk she caught her companion's eye resting thoughtfully upon her face and said impulsively, 'I'm sorry I made a fool of myself this evening. So very stupid of me.'

The professor smiled. The smile held mockery. 'Dear, oh, dear! Here we go again back to square one, about to discuss the weather, unless I am much mistaken, and I was beginning to think that we had at least cracked the ice.'

'I don't know what you mean...'

'Such a useful remark and quite without truth. Never mind, though, tell me about to-morrow—do you check us in as we arrive? Presumably we are expected to go to the hospital main entrance...'

She would have liked to have argued with him but he hadn't given her the chance. Besides, she mustn't forget that he was a visiting specialist, to be treated with respect. 'No need for that,' she told him. 'You can use the door we came through this evening. I'll be at the desk in the reception area, ticking off names.'

'Then what do you do?'

'Go to the kitchen and make sure that coffee and biscuits are ready, there's a buffet lunch at one o'clock, I'll have to see to that, and then the clearing-up afterwards and there's tea at four o'clock.'

'You have help, of course?'

'Oh, yes, I'm just there to see that everything is going smoothly.'

She finished the *bombe glacé* with a small sigh of content and he ordered coffee.

'Do you see much of young Derek?'

'Almost nothing, only if we happen to be at home at the same time and that's seldom. Is he a friend of yours? I mean, aren't you a bit...?' She stopped and went pink and he finished smoothly,

'Old for him. Of course I am; my father was a friend of his father. I've known the family on and off for a long time.'

'I didn't mean to be rude, I'm sorry.'

He shook his head slowly. 'Two apologies in less than half an hour, Beatrice. Don't do it again or I might have to alter my opinion of you.'

He passed his cup for more coffee and began to talk about her brother.

It was after eleven o'clock by the time he stopped the car by the passage door. 'You're not supposed to park here,' said Beatrice as he got out.

She might have saved her breath for he took no notice, but opened the door and followed her inside.

'Thank you for a very pleasant evening,' said Beatrice politely. 'It was most kind of you. Goodnight, Professor van der Eekerk.'

He began to walk up the stairs beside her and she said, 'There's no need.'

'Hush, girl, save your breath for the climb.' So she hushed since there was little point in arguing with him and at her door he took the key from her and stood aside to let her in and then went ahead of her to turn on the lights before wishing her a quiet goodnight and going down the stairs two at a time in what she considered to be a highly dangerous manner.

She stood in the middle of the room reflecting that when she had been taken out for the evening she had always been thanked for her company and been given to understand that her companion had enjoyed it—Professor van der Eekerk, on the other hand, hadn't said any such thing.

She had a bath and got ready for bed feeling peevish. 'There will be no need to speak to him tomorrow,' she told herself, and thumped her pillows into comfort. 'I dare say he only asked me out because he wanted company at the dinner-table and I happened to be handy.'

She went to sleep, having quite forgotten about Tom.

The learned gentlemen attending the seminar began to arrive soon after half-past eight and Beatrice was kept busy ticking their names off her list, helping the more elderly out of their coats and scarves, finding mislaid notes, spectacles and cough lozenges and ushering them into the conference hall, a gloomy place filled with rows of uncomfortable chairs, its walls painted a particularly repellent green and having a small platform at one end on which was a table, half a dozen chairs and, since Beatrice found the place so bleak, a bowl of hyacinths on the table, flanked by a carafe of water and a glass.

The first speaker was Professor Moore, still suffering from his cold and by no means in the best of tempers. Once he had arrived his colleagues started to file into the hall, stopping to greet friends as they went and taking their time about it. Beatrice looked at her list; there were still half a dozen to come...

They came in a group and one of them was Professor van der Eekerk, towering over his

companions. She noticed that he appeared to
be on the best of terms with all of them, and,
like them, greeted her with a polite good
morning before going into the hall. She wasn't
sure what she had expected; all she knew was
that she felt disappointed. She watched his
massive back disappear through the door and
told herself that she had no wish to see him
again. A wish she was unable to fulfil, for,
the first paper having been duly read and discussed, the distinguished audience surged out
of the hall and into one of the smaller lecture-
rooms where coffee and biscuits awaited them.
Still deep in talk, they received their cups and
saucers in an absentminded fashion, and
Beatrice, making her way from one group to
another with some of the biscuits, was sure
that Professor van der Eekerk was unaware
of her being there, deep as he was in discussion with several other doctors. She was
wrong, of course. His heavy-lidded gaze followed her around the room without apparently doing so and when she was at last back
behind the coffee percolators, refilling the
cups her helpers fetched, all she could see of
him was his back in a superbly tailored suit.

The second paper to be read before lunch
started late, which meant that it finished late.
Beatrice, pacifying the cook, wished the er-

udite and wordy gentleman on the platform to Jericho, going on and on about endocrinology. When he at length came to an end she lost no time in urging his audience to repair to the smaller lecture hall once more and ladled soup to be handed round without loss of time while the cook seethed over the lamb cutlets, ruined, she assured Beatrice.

Ruined or not, they were eaten; indeed, the various conversations were so engrossing that she doubted if anyone had noticed what was on their plates. She portioned out castle puddings with a generous hand and went to make sure that the coffee percolators were ready.

The afternoon session was to be taken up by a paper on haematology by Professor van der Eekerk and, contrary to the previous lecturer, she hoped that he would take a long time delivering it; it would give them time to clear the room once more and put out the tea things—sandwiches, buttered buns and fruit cake. Having some considerable experience of similar occasions, she knew what got eaten and what got left.

Ready and with time to spare, she took a discreet peep through the not quite closed doors of the lecture hall. Professor van der Eekerk was well into his subject: haemolytic anaemia, jaundice, the Rh factor and a lot of long words which meant nothing to her. She opened the door a little wider and listened. He had a deep voice, rather slow, and with only a trace of an accent. She poked her head round the door and he looked straight at her. Without a pause he went on, 'Now polycythaemia is an entirely different matter...'

Beatrice withdrew her head smartly. He had appeared to look at her but the hall was large and she had been right at the back of it. She thought it unlikely that he had noticed her. She glanced at her watch; he was due to finish in five minutes, so she and her helpers started to carry the plates of food in. With luck, no one would linger over tea, for they would all be anxious to go home. She sighed. They would be back again tomorrow.

Her hopes were dashed. They sat over their tea, drinking second and third cups and eating everything in sight. 'Like a swarm of locusts,' said the cook crossly, cutting up yet another cake. 'And 'ow they can eat and drink and talk about blood beats me though I must say 'e 'oo did the talking is something like. Wouldn't mind 'aving a lecture from 'im.' Beatrice, bearing the cake, was stopped by the senior medical consultant of the hospital. 'Very nice, Miss Crawley, organised with your usual finesse. We are a little behind time, I fancy, but Professor van der Eekerk's paper was most interesting. We look forward to his second talk tomorrow. Is that more cake? Splendid.' He beamed at her. 'A delightful tea—most enjoyable.'

They all went at last; Beatrice sent the part-time helpers home, spent a brief time with the cook checking the menu for the next day, assured her that she could manage on her own and, once left to herself, emptied the dishwasher and began to put out coffee-cups and saucers, spoons and sugar basins ready for the morning. They were well ahead for the next day, she reflected. There had been time while they waited between the breaks to prepare the food and collect plates and cutlery ready to lay the tables again. She had almost finished when the entrance door was pushed open and Tom came in.

'Thought you'd be here. Lord, I've had a busy day—I could do with a sandwich or even a coffee . . .'

Beatrice arranged the last few cups just so. 'Go away, Tom. I'm tired, I've had a busy day too and you know you have no business to be here.'

'Since when haven't I been allowed to come over here?' He was laughing, wheedling her.

'You know very well what I mean. Of course you can come here when you need to see the path. lab about something or other. But this isn't the path. lab and in any case if you are as busy as you say you are you can telephone.'

'Snappy, aren't you? Never mind, I'll make allowances, I dare say your dull old men have bored you stiff. When we marry you can stay at home and keep house and be a lady of leisure.'

'I'm not going to marry you, Tom. Now go away, do.'

He came round the counter towards her. 'Oh, come on, you know you don't mean it.'

He was smiling and he had a charming smile, only she didn't feel like being charmed; she wanted a quick meal, a hot bath and her bed. She pushed his arm away. 'I said go away...'

The outer door had opened very quietly. Professor van der Eekerk was beside her before she had even seen him come in. He said smoothly, 'Miss Crawley, do forgive me, but I need to check the times of the papers being read tomorrow. Perhaps you would like me to come back later?'

He smiled gently at her and glanced at Tom Ford, murmured something or other and turned to go again.

'Don't go,' said Beatrice, rather more loudly than she had intended. 'There's no need. I mean, I'll be glad to help you, Professor.' She shot a fiery look at Tom. 'Dr Ford was just going.'

'In that case...' observed the professor and held the door for Tom to go through, giving him a cheerful goodnight as he went.

'Now what?' asked Beatrice, very much on edge and not disposed to be polite or friendly.

'Food, a long hot bath and bed,' said Professor van der Eekerk, putting his finger exactly on the crux of the matter. 'Go and get a coat—don't bother with titivating yourself, you'll do as you are. We'll go to a fish and chip shop or something similar. You can eat your fill and be back here within the hour.'

'I had intended——' began Beatrice haughtily.

'Beans on toast? A boiled egg? A great girl like you needs a square meal. Off you go.'

He held the door open and after a moment she went past him and started up the stairs. She told herself that she hadn't said anything because she was speechless with rage; in actual fact he had suggested exactly what she wanted to do...

She got her coat and, since he had said—rudely, she considered—that she was all right as she was, she didn't bother to look in the mirror. When she joined him she said frostily, 'You wanted to ask me something, Professor?'

He looked vague. 'Did I? Oh, yes, of course. It was the first thing I thought of. I was coming out of the hospital when I saw your boyfriend coming this way...'

'He's not my boyfriend.'

'No, no, of course not.' He went around turning off lights and then ushered her out into the passage. 'I was told by your excellent head porter that there is a splendid café just along the street. Alfred's Place is its name, I believe—let us sample Alfred's cooking.'

He took her arm and marched her out of the forecourt and into the busy street, its small shops still open and plenty of people still about. The café was a bare five minutes' walk away; the professor pushed open the door and urged her inside. It was almost full and the air was redolent of hot food and Beatrice's charming nose wrinkled with delight as they sat down at a table in one corner.

There was no menu but Alfred came over at once. ''Ow do?' he greeted them cheerfully. 'Me old pal at St Justin's gave me a tinkle, said you might be coming. 'E's 'ead porter.'

'Very thoughtful of him. What can you offer us? We have very little time but we're hungry...'

'Pot o' tea ter start and while yer drinking it I'll do a couple of plates of bacon and eggs, tomatoes and fried bread.' Alfred, small and portly, drew himself up. 'I reckon you wouldn't eat better up west.'

'It sounds delicious.' The professor glanced at Beatrice. 'Or is there something else you fancy, Beatrice?'

'I can't think of anything nicer. And I'd love a cup of tea.'

The tea came, borne by a plump pretty girl, untidy, but nevertheless very clean. She gazed at the professor as she set the pot before Beatrice. 'Dad says you're a professor,' she breathed in an excited whisper. 'I never seen one before.'

She gave him a wide grin and hurried away to answer another customer.

'I feel that I should have horns or a beard and a basilisk stare at the very least!'

Beatrice poured their tea, a strong brew, powerful enough to revive the lowest spirits. 'Well, you do look like one, you know, only you're a bit too young...'

'I'll start the beard first thing tomorrow morning.'

'No, no, don't be absurd, what I mean is that most people think of professors as being elderly and grey-haired and forgetful and unworldly.'

'I have the grey hair, but I rather like the world, don't you? I can be forgetful when I want to be and in a few years I shall be elderly.'

'Rubbish,' said Beatrice. 'I don't suppose you are over forty.'

'Well, no, I'm thirty-seven—and how old are you, Beatrice?'

She answered without thinking. 'Twenty-eight,' and then, 'Why do you ask? It's really not polite...'

'But I'm not polite, only when life demands it of me. I wanted to know so that we can clear the air.'

'Clear the air—whatever do you mean?'

She wasn't going to find out for Alfred arrived with two plates piled high with crisp bacon, eggs fried to a turn and mushrooms arranged nicely on a bed of fried bread.

'Eat it while it's 'ot,' he told them, and took away the teapot to refill it.

Alfred was a good cook, perhaps the best in the area bisected by the Commercial Road. With yet more tea, they did justice to his food.

Beatrice put down her knife and fork. 'That was lovely. My goodness, I feel ready for anything.'

'Not until the morning. You're going back to bath and a bed now.'

He smiled at her protesting face. 'Doctor's orders.'

He paid the bill, added a tip to make Alfred's eyes glisten, assured him that they would certainly come again, and marched her out back at a brisk pace to her own door, opened it for her, bade her goodnight and closed it quietly, barely giving her time to thank him. Almost as though he couldn't wait to get away from her. Yet he had rescued her from Tom. She was too tired to think about it; she had her bath and got into bed and was asleep within minutes.

The first paper in the morning was to be read by an eminent surgeon from Valencia, well known for his research into nutritional disorders. It was a cold dark morning and his audience came promptly and briskly, glad to

be indoors. Beatrice, counting heads, saw that
they were all there. She hadn't seen Professor
van der Eekerk go in, but there he was sitting
near the front, his handsome head bent to
listen to whatever it was his neighbour had to
say. She went back to the kitchen and began
to pile biscuits on to plates and make sure that
there was a plentiful supply of coffee. There
was at least an hour before it would be required; she began to do her daily round of the
building, checking that everything was as it
should be. She had barely done that before it
was time to help with the coffee and once that
was done she went to her small office on the
ground floor, to do the paperwork which took
up a good deal of her time. Professor van der
Eekerk had begun his paper but this time she
didn't go near the lecture hall; she had too
much to do, she reminded herself, and besides that, what was the point? She didn't see
him to speak to for the rest of the day, and
somehow, she didn't quite know how, she
missed his leaving at the end of the afternoon. Leave-takings had been slow and
numerous and several people had stopped to
speak to her and thank her but he hadn't been
among them. Putting everything to rights
once more with the help of her assistants, she
reflected that probably, since they had met at

a friend's house, politeness had prompted him to seek her out; she was working at St Justin's after all and he couldn't have ignored her completely. He had, she thought, done rather more than that, and at least the sight of him might discourage Tom.

She made her supper in her little kitchenette and went to bed with a book. She read half a page and flung the book on to the floor. Life was being very dull, she decided, and she had to admit that she would miss Tom's company even though he could be tiresome. At least she had New Year's Eve to look forward to, she reminded herself. Derek's grandmother lived in Hampstead, a lively old lady who never missed an opportunity to enjoy life. His parents would be coming up to spend the night and he had managed somehow to be free. There would be a lot of people there and she mulled over her wardrobe.

Waking in the morning, common sense combined with the cold clear winter's day decided her to despatch the professor from her mind. It was surprising how sensible she felt about it; of course, after a day's work and feeling a bit fed up, she would probably regret not seeing him again.

Quite soon, she was summoned to the hospital committee's office. She went, outwardly composed, inwardly wondering what was in store for her. Like every other hospital St Justin's was cutting back on staff, beds and equipment—perhaps there was a plan to cut back on the research department, the path. labs and the numerous study rooms and library. If so, she supposed that they could make do with part-time staff although the lab people weren't going to like that . . . She went through the hospital and into a wide corridor at the front of the building where the various offices were, and tapped on a door, convinced that she was about to be made redundant.

A voice told her to enter and she went inside.

Ten minutes later she came out again; nothing was being cut back, she wasn't to be given her notice; on the contrary, she was to exchange her post with someone similar in the Netherlands. 'A step forward in the unification of Europe', she had been told. It was envisaged that within the next few years it would be possible for hospitals to exchange staff as and when they wished; this was by way of an experiment.

Her observation that she had no knowledge of the Dutch language was waved aside. 'English is spoken,' she was told, 'although of course you will be expected to study the language during your stay there.'

She had wanted to know how long that would be.

'We haven't decided yet. I believe that the Leiden School of Medicine recommend a month in the first instance. Two ward sisters, a male nurse and a physiotherapist will also be going.'

Authority had dismissed her courteously, her head full of unanswered questions.

That evening she phoned her mother, who heard her news without interruption and then remarked in her placid way, 'Well, dear, it will make a nice change for you and you'll meet some nice people. You might see that charming man who came to the party with Derek——'

'Most unlikely,' said Beatrice quickly, and wished that it wasn't. 'I'll see you tomorrow. I'll know more by then, maybe.'

She dressed with care on New Year's Eve in a silk crêpe dress in a pretty shade of old rose, covered it with a long velvet coat and, with her new shoes and her evening bag tucked under her arm, went down to the forecourt. It was a bitter night but the sky was clear and the hospital lights dispelled the dark. She was fitting the key in her car's lock when footsteps behind her made her turn round. Tom was coming towards her.

She had managed to avoid him for two days, firmly refusing to go out with him when he had telephoned. She opened the door and got into the car just as he reached it.

'Still playing hard to get?' he wanted to know. 'I'm not taking no for an answer, Beatrice.'

'I'm not playing at anything, Tom; I said no and I meant it.'

She switched on the engine and he put a hand on the window. 'Let's get together and talk this through,' he suggested. 'You know as well as I do that we could rub along together.'

'I'm sorry, Tom, but no.'

'Are you off this weekend?'

'I'm going home, Tom. I must go, I'm already late.'

He took his hand away reluctantly and she drove out into the quiet street and turned the car westward. The street would be lively enough in a few hours' time, the pub would be overflowing with people celebrating the new year and there would be a good deal of activity still. She drove carefully, avoiding the very heart of the city where crowds were already gathering. She wasn't nervous, only anxious to get to Hampstead on time.

The house Derek's grandmother lived in was in a quiet, wide avenue, a large Edwardian mansion surrounded by a well kept and uninteresting garden, full of laurel bushes and well kept shrubs, rather sombre. Its large windows were blazing with light and there were any number of cars parked on the sweep before the front door. Beatrice eased her little car between a Daimler and a Mercedes, replaced her sensible driving shoes with the new ones and trod across to the portico. The old lady lived in some style and her servants had been with her for almost all of her married life. The elderly butler who admitted her was white-haired and a little shaky but his appearance brought a nostalgic whiff of earlier days as he led her solemnly across the hall and handed her over to an equally elderly maid who preceded her up the long flight of stairs to the room set aside for lady guests. Beatrice poked at her hair, wriggled her feet in the shoes to make sure that they were comfortable, gave the maid the coat she had shed and went downstairs.

There was a good deal of noise coming from behind the big double doors on one side of the hall. The butler opened them for her and she went inside and found a room full of people.

It was necessary to find her hostess and she was relieved to see the old lady sitting at the other end of the room, talking to Derek. She made her way there, said all that was civil, exchanged a friendly kiss with Derek and looked around for her mother and father.

'They're in the second drawing-room; I've just come from there. Do come back here when you've spoken to them, I want to hear about this jaunt to Holland.'

She had begun to work her way through the groups of people drinks in hand chatting together. She knew several of them and stopped to say hello as she went. She was going through the open arch which led to a smaller similar room when she stopped.

Professor van der Eekerk was leaning against a wall, watching her.

CHAPTER THREE

BEATRICE felt a glow of pleasure at the sight of him and instantly suppressed it. She said sedately, 'Why, Professor, I didn't expect to see you here.'

He had moved to stand in front of her so that she wouldn't be able to pass unless she forgot her manners and poked him in the waistcoat. Unthinkable but tempting. 'Why should you expect to see me?' he asked coolly. 'How are you?'

'Very well, thank you. It will be nice when this cold weather——'

'Ah, yes, let us hide our true feelings behind remarks about the weather. Are you glad to see me?'

She gave him a cold glance. 'I would rather discuss the weather.'

He smiled suddenly. 'Come off your high horse, Beatrice, and tell me how life is treating you.'

She had quite forgotten her parents. 'Well, just the same as usual, you know.' She glanced at him and found him watching her intently so that she felt compelled to add, 'As a matter of fact, I have to go on an exchange scheme—just for a month or so—to promote a wider exchange of jobs in the EC.' She wasn't going to tell him where.

In the silence which followed she stared at his waistcoat, a sober black affair, not at all like the trendy sort of thing some of the men there were wearing. When she peeped at him at last he was obviously waiting for her to say something else. She said pettishly, 'Oh, all right, I'm to go to Holland.'

He said mildly, 'Yes, I know. Leiden—you'll like it there, I think. Why didn't you want to tell me, Beatrice?'

'It couldn't possibly interest you. Besides, it would look as though...'

He said gently, 'But I am not very often in Leiden; our chances of meeting would be very slight.'

She said, suddenly brisk, 'Well, that's all right, isn't it? Now I really must find Mother and Father. If I don't see you again...'

'Oh, but you will. I'm spending the weekend with Derek's people at Little Estling. You're going home tomorrow?'

She had said yes before she had time to think.

'Splendid; I'll drive you down. I have to be back on Sunday evening—I can give you a lift back.'

'I intended driving down in my own car.'

'No, no, that won't do at all; I can tell you about the hospital at Leiden as we go.'

He smiled down at her and she said weakly, 'Oh, very well. Now I really must...'

'Yes, yes, they are at the far end of the room. Let us join them.'

Her mother offered a cheek for her to kiss. 'That's a pretty dress, darling.' Mrs Crawley eyed her daughter with motherly concern. 'What's all this about going to Holland?' She smiled at the professor as she spoke. 'I expect you know about it, Gijs?'

Gijs, indeed. Beatrice waited to see what he would say.

'Yes, I was told something of the scheme when I was in Leiden this week. I'm looking forward to meeting the nursing staff who will be going over too. I feel it is most important that we should have instant rapport with those with whom we work wherever we go.'

'I'm sure you're right,' said Mrs Crawley comfortably. 'I don't suppose you will see anything of Beatrice, then.'

'Not very likely, I'm afraid, but she will find everyone very friendly and there's quite a pleasant social life in the hospital and medical school and the usual free time, I believe. You and Dr Crawley might spend a weekend while she is there; Leiden is a charming city and its centre is still unspoilt.'

'That's an idea. Are you staying in town or going to Derek's people this weekend?'

'I'm driving down early tomorrow morning. I'll bring Beatrice with me for I have to get back at the same time as she does.'

'I haven't decided——' began Beatrice, put out at the way things were being arranged just as though she weren't there.

'What a splendid idea,' said her mother. 'I don't suppose you'll be able to have coffee with us but do spend half an hour in the evening when you come for Beatrice. My husband wants to know about the seminar last week.' She looked round her. 'Where is he?'

'I'll go and find him,' said Beatrice rather coldly. Once again she regretted her inability to flounce.

There was a splendid buffet supper and several people she knew to gossip with. She piled a plate and joined some friends and presently someone started the music and she put down her plate and danced off with Derek.

'Where's this fellow Tom? Didn't you bring him with you? Everyone is welcome at Granny's, you know.'

'I—that is, I've given him up.'

'That's great. Never liked the fellow. After a wife with the necessary to give him a leg-up, was he?'

'Since you put it that way, yes.'

'Gave him the right-about, did you?'

'Yes, only he won't...'

'Pestering you? Want me to sort him out?'

'No, no, Derek, that would never do. Besides, this exchange business will do the trick. I'll be gone for at least a month, maybe as long as three—he'll find someone else by the time I get back.'

'OK, but I don't want to see you put upon.'

'Now that is nice of you, Derek, but girls who get put upon are size eight with big blue eyes and golden hair and figures like lead pencils.'

'What are you, love? Size eighteen with vital statistics to match?'

'Don't be vulgar, Derek, I'm size...' She closed her mouth with a snap; the music had stopped and Professor van der Eekerk was at her elbow.

'Well, go on, tell,' said Derek, 'we're both dying to know.'

'*No.*'

'I dare say Gijs will worm it out of you—
I must go and do a duty dance with an aunt,
I suppose.' He patted her on the shoulder in
a brotherly fashion and went off into the
people milling around them. Beatrice was
thinking of something cool and polite to say
before slipping away herself when the music
started and she found herself dancing again,
this time with the professor. He danced very
well.

'Don't worry your head trying to think of
a way of snubbing me politely.' His voice was
placid and a little amused. 'I've been around
for long enough to guess your size without
having to ask you.'

She gave a choking gasp. 'You're outra-
geous—aren't you supposed to be a gentleman?' She was aware as she uttered this that
it was the kind of remark a Victorian miss
might have made—a mealy-mouthed little
prig in a crinoline.

He said mildly, 'I'm a haematologist, and
I do believe that I told you that I like to speak
my mind but if it will soothe you we will
discuss the weather.'

She found herself smiling. 'You're ridic-
ulous and I'm sorry if I was priggish. I'm
rather on the large side...' She glanced down

at her magnificent person with an unself-conscious look which brought a smile to the professor's thin mouth. 'I've always wanted to be small and slender and golden-haired and helpless—you know, the kind of girl who's frightened of spiders and doesn't know how to change a plug and expects men to carry things for her.'

'You, of course, can change a plug and pick up spiders and carry things for yourself.' He wasn't even smiling, just looking soothing.

'Well, yes, I can. Are you at St Justin's again?'

'Just for a couple of days. I've several cases to see at Bristol and a couple at Liverpool.'

'Then you go back to Holland?'

'Briefly. I have to go to Chicago very shortly.'

'You don't have much time at home, do you?' She glanced up at him and he smiled a little.

'I wish I had more; now that Alicia is older she misses me.'

'Alicia?'

'My daughter. My wife died six years ago. Alicia is almost seven years old.'

'I'm sorry—about your wife I mean. You must be glad to have a little girl to look after.'

'I'm afraid that I haven't done much of that, although we have great fun when I am at home. She has an excellent nanny and of course she goes to school now.'

'You should marry again...' Beatrice went a very bright red. 'Oh, I do beg your pardon, that was very rude of me, only the thought popped into my head.'

He said gravely, 'Don't apologise. I intend to marry again.'

'How nice,' said Beatrice quite inadequately. The evening was suddenly flat; she wished she hadn't come—then she wouldn't have known and they might have got more friendly. Fortunately she wasn't likely to see him again. Well, tomorrow, of course—she could hardly back out of going down to Little Estling with him—but that, she promised herself, would be the very last time. She began to talk then, light chatter suitable for party conversation, and, when the music stopped, smiled at him and slipped away into the other room and lost herself in the crowd there.

The party gathered momentum until everyone fell quiet, as, with champagne glasses in hand, they listened to the first stroke of Big Ben and then began a round of greetings and kissing and "Happy New Year"'s. Beatrice, going from one guest to the next, found herself in front of the professor. 'A Happy New Year,' she wished him, and made to pass on.

A large gentle hand detained her. 'And to you, Beatrice. I wonder where we shall be in a year's time?'

She gave him a quick glance. 'Probably I'll be here and you'll be in Holland—so much can happen in a year.'

'Indeed, yes. I anticipate a most interesting twelve months.'

'Yes, well, I dare say, especially if you're going to get married.' She added awkwardly, 'I'd better finish my round—to greet everyone, you know.'

She left him standing there, wishing she could have stayed and talked to him. She didn't speak to him again, only to nod agreement to his suggestion that he should call for her at half-past eight the next morning.

It was a bitterly cold morning, and she got into a thick tweed skirt, a shirt-blouse with an angora sweater in a warm russet and a leaf-brown top coat, stuffed a woolly cap and gloves into a pocket, found her shoulder-bag and hurried down to the forecourt. The Bentley was there and the professor got out as she reached it, opened her door with a cheerful good morning and shut it again.

'Did you sleep well?' he asked her as he got in beside her.

'Yes, but not for long enough. I very nearly turned over and went to sleep again.'

'I'm glad you didn't—it's a long climb to your flat.'

She turned to look at him and he went on cheerfully, 'I would have banged on your door and made sure that you got dressed.'

'You wouldn't...'

The look he gave her was slightly mocking. 'I would. Are you warm enough? Not forgotten anything? Good, we should be there in time for coffee.'

The London streets were almost empty, midnight revellers still in their beds and no one going to work. They drove without hindrance through the city, joined the M40 and sped along the motorway while the professor kept up a gentle flow of talk about nothing in particular. His quiet undemanding voice and the warm comfort of the car were very soothing. Beatrice could have fallen asleep with the greatest of ease but she resisted the temptation.

'You were going to tell me about Leiden,' she reminded him.

'A delightful place—old and picturesque, full of narrow alleys and cobbled streets. The houses vary from rows of miniature cottages with gabled roofs to patrician houses beside the canals. I believe that you will enjoy exploring them. There are half a dozen museums, all interesting, and also some excellent antiques shops.' He glanced sideways at her. 'There are plenty of other shops too and of course den Haag and Amsterdam are easily reached.'

'I don't suppose you would know what hours I work or when I would be free?'

'Roughly the same as here and more to your advantage, I should imagine. Leiden is very compact—ten minutes' walk would take you from the medical school to the shopping streets.'

'You know Leiden well?'

'I was at the medical school there before I came over here . . .'

'You've got Dutch and English degrees?'

'Yes. You will have no difficulty with the language. Everyone speaks English—that is, everyone who you are likely to meet. You will be offered lessons in Dutch if you wish.'

'Will you be going back to Holland soon?'

'Within the next few days. I shan't be in Holland for some time, though.'

'You're going to America . . . will you have time to see Alicia before you go?'

'Oh, yes. There is always time to do something one wants to do.'

She opened her mouth and closed it again; she had asked a great many questions. They were off the motorway now, driving towards Thame and then turning off into a country road. Even in midwinter the country looked beautiful. The frost lay thick on the fields and hedges and the trees, bare of leaves, were silhouetted against the grey sky. The professor turned the car into the narrow lane and looked at the clock on the dashboard. Minutes later the village came into sight. There was no one about but smoke rose from the chimneys; it looked like a picture postcard.

Her home, a nice old place, built upon and added to over the years, looked very welcoming, and as the professor stopped the car the front door opened, and the doctor, preceded by an elderly Labrador, came out.

'Dead on time,' he declared. 'Your mother has just this minute taken the mince pies out of the oven.' He kissed his daughter and offered his hand to the professor. 'You'll come in for a cup of coffee?'

'Much as I would like to, I mustn't stop— I promised Derek's people that I would be with them as soon after ten o'clock as possible.' He glanced at Beatrice. 'I'll come for Beatrice tonight—perhaps we might have a talk then. Mrs Crawley told me that you were interested in the seminar.'

'Splendid. I'll look forward to that. We'll see you then.'

They watched him drive away, back through the village and beyond to Derek's home. 'A good chap,' commented Dr Crawley. 'Did you have a pleasant drive here?'

They went into the house and Beatrice went straight to the kitchen, throwing her coat on to the settle in the hall as she went.

Her mother greeted her warmly. 'He said last night that he wouldn't be able to stop this morning—is he coming for you later?'

Beatrice sat down at the kitchen table and took a mince pie. She put an arm round Nobby, who had followed her into the house. 'Yes, he didn't say when.'

'It'll be quite late—they're having a dinner party—I know because Sybil phoned to ask if we'd all go—it's a spur-of-the moment affair. You don't mind not going, darling? But we see so little of you and we wanted to hear about this Dutch job. They're dining at seven o'clock because Gijs has to drive back to

London, so I should think he would not be here much before nine, would you?'

Her mother had sat down at the table opposite to her, the coffee-pot between them.

'I don't mind a bit,' said Beatrice, and poured coffee for her father. 'I don't know much about going to Holland—you know how it is; authority sends for you and tells you something and takes it for granted that you know all the details, but I shouldn't think it would be for a week or two.'

'All the same, it might be a good idea to look over your clothes. I wonder if you will go out at all? And will you see much of Gijs?'

'I don't think so. He said he was hardly ever in Leiden and he's going to America very shortly.' She sounded very casual. 'He's a widower, did you know? He has a little daughter...' Beatrice took a bite of mince pie and said through a full mouth. 'He's going to get married again.'

Her mother's gentle face hid a profound disappointment. 'Well, of course that would be the sensible thing to do—the poor child must miss her mother.'

'I believe Alicia was only a year or so old when she...' Beatrice paused. 'I don't know what happened to her.'

'We must wish him happy. Now do tell us
nything else you know about going to
eiden.'

'You'll like it,' interposed her father. 'I was
here for several months just after I qual-
fied—a charming place. I must bring your
1other over for a few days—I dare say we'll
e able to see something of you?'

They talked about it for some time until her
1other declared that she must cast an eye over
er cooking. 'Another turkey, darling,' she
xplained. 'Your father was given two, one
rom Biggs's Farm—you remember old Biggs
ad that mild stroke? And the other from the
Aitchells—your father helped them deliver a
ifficult calf a few weeks ago. The vet was
way and he was there anyway, taking a look
t Mrs Mitchell's varicose veins.' She gave the
ird an exploratory poke with a fork and
opped it back into the oven. 'George rang
his morning. The poor boy is working very
ard.'

'He's doing quite well,' said Dr Crawley.
Once he's qualified he can spend a year or
wo doing whatever he wants before he joins
1e and takes over later.'

The rest of the day, as far as Beatrice was
oncerned, was bliss; pottering around the
ouse, spending an hour with her mother,

going through the clothes in her wardrobe
some of which she might decide to take with
her. She took Nobby for a walk too, ate an
enormous lunch and then sat by the fire, half
asleep, carrying on a comfortable conver
sation devised to allow her to catch up on all
the local gossip.

It was after seven o'clock when she and her
mother went to get the supper. The turkey had
been magnificent hot, now they sliced it cold,
made sandwiches and more coffee and took
the tray back to the drawing-room. They
made a leisurely meal sitting round the fire
replenishing the coffee pot and crunching the
celery Beatrice had found in the fridge. She
had her splendid teeth in an apple when the
doorbell echoed down the flagstoned hall.

'Too soon,' said Beatrice, and looked at her
watch. 'Oh, lord, no, it isn't—it's almost nine
o'clock... I'll go.'

She opened the door, the apple still in her
hand. Professor van der Eekerk's bulk seemed
to fill the entire porch and his voice came from
way above her head. 'At a loss for words? No
remarks about the weather tripping off your
tongue, Beatrice? You appear surprised, or
am I perhaps mistaking that for something
else?'

'How you do talk,' she said crossly. 'Good evening, Professor, do come in.'

She shut the door behind him and led the way to the drawing room where he was welcomed warmly, offered coffee, and invited to sit down.

'You can spare half an hour, I hope?' enquired her mother. 'Beatrice, will you fill the coffee-pot, dear, and bring some of those little cheese savouries?' She looked across at their guest. 'You have had dinner, Gijs?'

'Thank you, yes, but I should like a cup of coffee—I'm in no great hurry and Beatrice isn't quite ready, is she?'

'We had a picnic supper round the fire—there was so much to talk about.'

Beatrice came back with the coffee and the cheese savouries and heard her father say, 'Splendid; I should like to hear what you thought of the seminar. Tell me, what was your opinion...?'

The two men were soon deep in serious discussion and presently Beatrice slipped out of the room and upstairs to get her things. She sat on the bed and finished her apple, feeling put out. Why was it that the professor always managed to make her feel awkward, even childish? She was neither; she held down a difficult job, got on well with the people she

worked with, had friends and led a pleasan
if busy life. She had begun to think of herself
as a career girl, independent, earning enough
money to enjoy her life, confident of her
future. So why, when she was with the pro
fessor, did she have doubts about it? She
didn't attempt to answer that, aware in her
heart of hearts that she had no desire to be a
career woman. She would like to be married
with a home to look after, children and a
husband who adored her. She wanted to cook
and sew and knit and make jam and do all
the things housewives did, but only if she met
the right man...

She sighed, collected her things and went
back to the drawing-room.

It was almost another hour before the pro
fessor glanced across to where she was sitting
chatting with her mother and wanted to know
if she was ready. For all the world as though
he had been sitting there patiently waiting for
her.

'Quite ready,' she told him coldly and put
on her coat, embraced her mother, kissed her
father, hugged Nobby too and went with him
to the car.

'That's a nice dog,' observed the professor
as he drove away.

So it was to be small talk. 'Yes, he is—we have two cats too—one of them, Muffin, for the time being is living in the airing cupboard with her kittens. It's warm there and quiet.'

He received this bit of information with a non-committal grunt and she cast around for some other topic of conversation.

'I expect you had a pleasant day?'

His yes was hardly encouraging but she tried again, 'Little Estling is a pretty village, isn't it?'

She glanced at him. His profile was without expression but she had the feeling that he was laughing. She sat up straight. 'All right,' she snapped, 'if you don't want to talk, say so.'

He gave her a quick blue stare. 'That's better. Of course I want to talk; I was just waiting for you to get the social chit-chat off your chest.'

'I don't know what you mean...'

'Now don't start again. Tell me, do you know anything about Holland?'

'Well...' she considered for a moment. 'Not much. It's flat and there are a lot of canals and windmills and there's a famous flower market and a great many gabled houses.' She looked sideways and saw his smile. 'That's not much use, is it?'

'I will send you one or two books. Read
them carefully, Beatrice, then you will have
some idea of what to expect: the food, laws,
social services, very like your own country and
yet different.'

'Thank you, but can't I get the books here
and save you the trouble?'

'No. I'll have them sent to you. Now, tell
me, have you managed to fend off Tom's
advances?'

'I think so.' She sounded doubtful. 'And
I'll be going away...'

'If,' said the professor deliberately, 'he is
as devoted to you as he says, he will wait for
you to return—he might even go over to
Holland to see you.'

'He won't know where I am.'

'My dear girl, if a man is in love with a girl
he will make it his business to know where she
is.'

'Well, he can't be in love with me.' She
added with a flash of temper, 'He ate all the
sandwiches—well, he left me one, but what's
that to someone of my size?'

'Totally inadequate,' said the professor
gravely. 'Have you a busy week before you?'

'No, just the normal work. I dare say some
of the path. labs will be working late. If they

lo I make coffee and take them biscuits or
andwiches.'

'I shall be back at St Justin's in two days'
ime—may I take you out to dinner on
Wednesday evening? About seven-thirty, or
ater if you wish.'

'Thank you, I'd like that, but nearer eight
o'clock, please, in case I have to see to the
path. labs.'

'Of course.'

They were threading through the outskirts
of London, the streets as quiet as they had
been that morning. She glanced at her watch
and saw that it was well after eleven o'clock;
the day had gone so quickly. So, for that
matter, had the drive back.

The streets might be quiet but there was the
usual bustle in the hospital forecourt: two
ambulances unloading patients and the ac-
cident-room lights blazing. The professor
drove round the forecourt to the back of the
hospital and stopped before the door to the
research centre and path. labs.

'Thank you for the lift,' said Beatrice, and
started to get out of the car. 'I hope you have
good trips to Bristol and Liverpool.' She put
her hand on the door-handle and had it gently
lifted off again. 'Not so fast,' said the pro-

fessor, and got out, fetched her bag from the boot and opened her door.

She got out and put out a hand for her bag. 'Don't let me keep you...'

He locked the car and opened the door and followed her upstairs until they reached her own door, when he took the key from her and opened it and switched on the light.

The place looked cold and unwelcoming, despite the attempts she had made to brighten it up with lampshades and cushions. He switched on more lights, bent to light the gas fire and put down her bag.

'I'll see you on Wednesday evening,' he said quietly. 'Goodnight, Beatrice.'

He had gone, shutting the door gently behind him before she could reply.

She should have offered him coffee, she frowned. If only he didn't go away so abruptly she would have had the chance to ask. It was again as though he couldn't get away fast enough.

She pottered round, putting things ready for the morning. He couldn't dislike her all that much, since he had asked her out to dinner. Probably he was just interested in this scheme to exchange hospital personnel. There was no point in thinking about it, she told herself bracingly; she had better go to bed. Tomorrow was Monday...

It was Tuesday in the late afternoon when she was sent for to go to the hospital manager's office, to be told that arrangements had been made for her to travel to Leiden with the rest of the party in ten days' time. Her Dutch counterpart would arrive on the previous day so that she could be shown her work and given any necessary details.

'A day won't be long enough,' said Beatrice bluntly.

She was told to give her reasons, something which she did in a few succinct sentences.

'Yes, well, perhaps we might arrange for her to come a day earlier. The situation will not arise in your case, Miss Crawley; there will be someone cognisant with your work there to show you the ropes.' He gave her a bland smile. 'If you have any further questions...?'

'Yes—off duty? Salary? To whom am I responsible? Is our journey there to be arranged or must we see to it ourselves?'

The hospital manager coughed. 'Dear me, such a lot of questions.' But he answered them all the same, adding, 'It might be a good idea if you all got together before you go. Good evening to you, Miss Crawley.'

She had a phone call a little later that evening from the ward sister who was to go and arranged to meet her at some stage and the rest of the party too. 'It had better be soon,' said Sister Watts. 'I'm not sure what clothes to take, and what about money?'

'We'll talk about it. There'll be time to fix everything up before we go.'

Beatrice put the phone down and it rang again almost immediately.

'I've booked a table for half-past eight at the Connaught,' said Professor van der Eerkerk without wasting time on saying hello.

She said in a pointed manner, 'Good evening, Professor. That sounds delightful. At what time shall I expect you?'

'Just before eight o'clock. I'll come up.' His goodbye was austere.

'He could at least have sounded pleased at the idea of taking me out,' said Beatrice, addressing the silent phone. 'Now what shall I wear tomorrow?'

She had several suitable dresses spread out on the divan when the doorbell rang. She went to answer it, prudently leaving the chain up. One of the hospital porters was standing there with a parcel under his arm.

'Just handed in, Miss Crawley, with instructions to let you have it at once.'

She thanked him and took it into her room and unwrapped it—two books. One, from its title, she took to be a modern history of the Netherlands together with its customs and habits; the second apparently dealt with its constitution, laws and politics. Heavy reading, but it had been kind of the professor to send them. Reading about customs and habits and the Dutch way of life would be interesting. She wasn't too sure about the second book.

She went back to the important task of choosing what to wear on the following evening.

She was on her way up to her flat after making sure that everything was all right and that the path. people who were still working had all that they wanted when she came face to face with Tom.

He greeted her with a charming smile. 'Darling Beatrice, I've an hour or two off duty. Let's go somewhere and have a drink and talk things over.'

She paused one foot on the stairs. 'Hello, Tom. I'm going out this evening and I wish I could make you understand that there's nothing to talk over. Not any more. Do please understand that.'

She went past him and he started to follow her. She went on upstairs and then stopped. 'Go away, do. I shall be late.'

'I must see you—explain—before you go to Holland.' He smiled again, turning on all the charm.

'Well, you can't. Tom, why can't you understand that I don't want to marry you? Why do you persist?'

'Because I know you'll change your mind, darling—women do, you know.'

'Well, here's one who won't.' She swept on upstairs, opened her door and shut it firmly behind her.

She wasn't going to let him spoil her evening, she told herself as she showered and got into the midnight-blue velvet dress she had decided to wear. Ready with only a few moments to spare, she studied herself in the mirror. The dress was just right with its long tight sleeves and demure neckline. She added a plain gold chain, checked her evening bag, crammed her tired feet into the new shoes and tossed her velvet coat over a chair just as the doorbell rang.

She opened the door at once, only remembering at the last minute that it might be Tom. It must have shown on her face, for the pro-

fessor gave her a considered look as he went
past her.

'Who were you expecting? Surely, even at
my worst, I don't bring such a look of annoyance to your face?'

CHAPTER FOUR

BEATRICE said breathlessly, 'Oh, I'm so glad it's you.' She put a hand on his arm and he took it in his own firm hand. 'So silly,' she went on, 'only Tom—I saw him earlier this evening and I remembered just as I opened the door that it might be him...'

He looked down at her, his face calm, almost placid. 'He's been bothering you again? I begin to think that he loves you after all.'

She shook her head. 'No, I'm sure he doesn't—he said—however, never mind what he said. I'm sorry to make a fuss.'

'It's a pity that I am returning to Holland in the morning.'

She smiled then. 'Please don't worry—I'm quite able to look after myself, you know.'

His placid agreement rather annoyed her.

He helped her on with her coat and then they went down to the car together, with Beatrice doing her best not to search the fore-court for signs of Tom. There was no sign of

him and she got into the car with a small sigh
of relief, something which her companion
noted with faint amusement. He made no
comment however, but talked of this and that
as he drove westward through the city until
they reached the West End, Carlos Place and
the Connaught Hotel.

Getting ready for bed hours later, Beatrice
went over the evening minute by minute. It
had been a success, there was no doubt of
that. Dinner had been superb in one of the
two restaurants in the hotel, quiet but not too
quiet, warm, the surroundings traditional and
at the same time luxurious. Beatrice, a girl
with a healthy appetite, ate fresh lobster
mousse, rosettes of lamb with a madeira sauce
with a delicious assortment of vegetables, followed by a biscuit *glacé* with raspberries and
praline, and as they ate they talked; it was
surprising what a great deal they had in
common although she had to admit with
hindsight that the professor had skilfully
evaded her tentative questions about himself,
generalising about life in his country without
once giving her a hint as to his own life. They
had wished each other goodnight at the door
of her flat and he had gone away with the
abruptness she had come to expect. Only it
would have been nice if he had suggested—

even hinted—at a future meeting. After all, she would be in the same town as he, even if he only went there from time to time. He had wished her a happy stay in Leiden, that had been all. She owned to disappointment but since it was late and she was tired she didn't dwell on it.

There was plenty to keep her occupied throughout the next few days; she spent an evening with Sister Watts, a young woman, younger than herself, small, dark and attractive. They agreed as to what clothes they should take with them, how much money they might need and that they would meet in the entrance hall of the hospital a few minutes before they were due to leave. The rest of the party would meet them at Heathrow, driving there in the charge nurse William Pearson's car. This nicely settled, Beatrice drove herself home on the Saturday afternoon and spent a blissful day doing nothing much. It was one of those unexpected days in winter when spring gave everyone a small taste of what was to come—blue skies and sunshine, albeit chilly. It spilled over into Sunday too and she took Nobby for a walk after church and then drove her parents over to Derek's home for tea. He wasn't there; if he had been she would have asked him if he knew anything about the professor, and his parents didn't mention him. It was her mother who remarked as they were driving home, 'A pity we shan't be seeing any more of your professor, darling. George wanted to meet him.'

'He's not my professor, Mother, dear,' said Beatrice, a little too quickly.

Back at the hospital with only three more days before she left, she sorted out her things ready to pack, sitting up in bed at night to read the books he had sent her. She had enjoyed the first one; it was interesting reading about other people's likes and dislikes in food, their houses, their clothes, their children's education—the second book she was finding harder, since it was about politics and laws and currency, but she plodded on, feeling that it was the least she could do since he had taken the trouble to let her have them.

The Dutch woman sent to replace her was no longer young, but she had a pleasant face and appeared very capable. Moreover her English was good and she had no difficulty in understanding the routine she would follow. They spent the day together, while she shadowed Beatrice's every movement, looked in cupboards and closets, was introduced to those of the staff who were working and then was ushered in and out of the various departments. Beatrice, aghast at the idea of introducing Juffrouw Winkelhuisen to endless pathologists and their underlings, was relieved when that lady suggested that it might be easier if everyone called her Ellie.

'I hope I settle down as easily as you have, Ellie,' said Beatrice on the last evening. 'Your English is so good and I don't know a word of Dutch.'

'That is not important, and I think that you will like it in Leiden, just as I like it here.' She smiled. 'We will write to each other?'

'Yes, let's do that. I'll say goodbye now, because I have to be over in the hospital by half-past seven tomorrow morning.'

There had been no sign of Tom. Beatrice went to bed early and presented herself and her luggage in the entrance hall with a couple of minutes to spare. The taxi was already there; she had been bidden goodbye on the evening before and now that the moment had come she wanted to be off. She had to wait five minutes for Sister Watts, who finally came racing along, clutching an assortment of scarves, handbag and umbrella.

'I'm late,' she said breathlessly, 'so sorry.' She beamed at Beatrice. 'I'm so excited. What's your opposite number like? Mine's delightful—took to the place like a fish to water.'

'So did mine,' said Beatrice. 'I only hope we'll do the same.'

They were in Schiphol almost before they had got used to the plane and once there they kept together, mindful of their instructions that they would be met and driven to Leiden where Beatrice was to stay, and then the others would go on to Utrecht and finally to Amsterdam.

Getting down from the minibus which had met them, she felt a sudden loneliness as it pulled away and she waved to her erstwhile companions. They had talked of meeting up but no plans could be made until they each knew their circumstances. She turned to find a porter standing by her.

It was a pleasant surprise when he said, 'Good day, miss,' and picked up her cases and led her through the entrance of the hospital. The surroundings were everything she might have expected of Holland: a canal bridged at intervals, with a broad street on either side lined by massive buildings which she took to be all part and parcel of the medical school. Inside the hospital wasn't much different from St Justin's—a high ceiling upheld by pillars, walls whose panels separated the paintings of dead and gone benefactors and, beneath these, just as at St Justin's, were plinths set at regular intervals, each with a stern-visaged gentleman atop it. Surgeons and physicians, she supposed, all looking exactly alike.

The porter led her to a booth at one side of the hall, behind which stood a stout man wearing an air of self-importance. He wished her good day and advised her in heavily accented English that the director of the hospital would be with her in a moment and enquired politely as to her journey.

'Most enjoyable,' said Beatrice, 'and so quick.'

The head porter looked over her shoulder and she turned round to see who it was—a tall, thin man with a stoop and a great deal of white hair. He offered a hand. 'Bernard ter Vosse, Miss Crawley. Welcome to our hospital; we are delighted to have you. I am the director, to whom you may apply if you need advice or help. There is also a directrice—you would say matron, I believe—who will give you her support.'

He nodded at the porter and spoke to him and the man picked up her case and crossed the hall to go through a door at the far end.

'He takes your bags to your room, but now you will please come with me and drink coffee and meet those for whom you will work.'

It was, she supposed, a committee-room of some sort, just now fairly full of people. She was introduced to them all in turn, trying to remember the names as they uttered them; these were the laboratory staff, the research staff and the heads of the various specialist units attached to the medical school. She was left finally with a girl of her own age who had been detailed to explain her work to her.

'Hetty Zilstra,' she said, offering a hand. 'As soon as this is over I'll show you your room and then we can spend the rest of the day looking round.'

Her English was excellent and Beatrice said so. 'I'd like to learn a little Dutch while I'm here, but it sounds difficult.'

Hetty laughed. 'It is, but of course you'll pick up enough to get you to the shops and sightseeing. All the profs speak English and I should think all their assistants do too. You haven't met any of them before, have you?'

'Well, I don't know if Professor van der Eekerk is ever here? I've met him at St Justin's.'

'Our Gijs.' Hetty rolled big blue eyes. 'Is he not a splendid man? I am—how do you

say?—betrothed, otherwise I would wish him
for myself. You too?'

'He's very nice,' said Beatrice cautiously.

'He can have any girl, like that.' Hetty
snapped her fingers. 'But he is...' She
frowned, seeking the right word. 'Impervi-
ous?'

'That will do very nicely,' said Beatrice.
Whatever she had intended to say didn't get
said, for the director joined them. 'So you
have met everyone, Miss Crawley? Now you
shall go with our good Hetty and see your
room and your workplace.'

'Do I have to shake hands again?' asked
Beatrice in a whisper.

'That is the custom,' said Hetty, 'but you
need only to smile.'

So Beatrice smiled and shook hands and
presently followed Hetty back into the entrance hall and down a side-corridor. It was
wide and long with windows overlooking the
canal and at its end they turned a corner into
a passage which led them to the back of the
vast place.

'Here is your workplace,' said Hetty,
waving an arm towards the wing running at
right angles to the main building, 'and on the
top floor there are the rooms for the profs—

hey are in the front of the hospital. I do not
now if it is bigger than your own hospital?'

'Much bigger,' said Beatrice, remembering
ow how certain her replacement had been
bout coping—this place was twice the size.
he would worry about that later; first her
wn quarters.

They were on the top floor, tucked away at
he end of a short corridor—a small sitting-
oom, an equally small bedroom, a shower-
oom and a beautifully equipped little kitch-
nette. The furniture was comfortable and the
vindows overlooked the back of the main
uilding.

She put her shoulder-bag down on the bed
nd observed, 'This is very nice.'

'It is necessary that you are comfortable for
ou must work hard.' Hetty straightened a
old in the bedspread. 'It is now time for the
rood maaltijd—lunch. I will sit here in your
itting-room while you do what you wish in
he bedroom and we will go together.'

It was all really rather fun, thought
Beatrice, following her new friend back to the
round floor and down another long passage
o the canteen.

She took her tray, piled her plate with bread
nd butter and cheese and a salad, a glass of
nilk and an apple, and sat down beside Hetty

at one of the tables. 'Do I come here each
day?'

'For your lunch, yes, but your breakfas
you make for yourself, also your evening mea
unless you want to come here and then yo
must tell one of the women at the counter.'

'Will I have time to shop?'

'Oh, yes, the shops are ten minutes' walk
You begin work at eight o'clock in th
morning and have an hour and a half for you
midday meal—that is the time to shop if yo
wish. One week you have Saturday free an
the other, Sunday, and also in the midweel
if it is convenient you may have an afternoon.

They ate for a time in silence then Hett
said, 'Now I will show you where you wil
work.'

The laboratories and research centre wer
large, well planned and splendidly equipped
No staffing problems, said Hetty, althoug
the hours might be erratic from time to time
'It depends on the professors,' she explained
'and what they're doing. Come and check th
equipment for cleaning and the cutlery an
the china.'

'Where will you be?' asked Beatrice.

'I am to go to Utrecht; the supervisor ther
is ill so I go to do her work.'

'You'll like that?'

'It will be all right, but I like Leiden best.
You will like to see it also.'

That would remain to be seen, reflected
Beatrice, but she hoped so.

They had tea then; Beatrice made it in her
little kitchenette and when they had drunk it
Hetty said, 'I go now. I must leave in the
morning but if you want me this evening you
may telephone the directrice. You are free now
until the morning. Why do you not go to the
shops and buy bread for your breakfast if you
wish to have it here.'

'Won't the shops be shut?'

'At six o'clock, but it is only about ten
minutes' walk. I will come with you.'

In her outdoor things once more, Beatrice
met Hetty in the entrance hall and walked the
short distance to the main street. The
Rapenburg, even in the dusk of a winter's day,
looked beautiful, but she had to admit that
the lighted shop windows were welcoming and
cheerful. Hetty took her to a small super-
market, gave her a wire basket and waited patiently while she found tea and sugar, bread,
butter and eggs and a carton of milk. It was
as easy as shopping in the Commercial Road
and more fun. She handed over her Dutch
guldens, got back a handful of small change
and, laden with a plastic shopping bag, went

back to the hospital with Hetty. If she had been on her own she might have been tempted to explore further along the street, but Hetty probably had her own plans for the evening; besides, there would be other days.

They said goodbye and Beatrice went to her flat, put away her groceries and unpacked. Early to bed, she decided; tomorrow would be a long day.

It was long but it was fun too. Her team of cleaners were all older women with only a smattering of English between them—nevertheless, they managed to tell Beatrice anything she wanted to know and the morning went well enough. After her midday meal in the canteen, eaten at a table where four girls were sitting, all of whom shook her hand and smiled in a friendly fashion, she nipped smartly out to the shops once more.

This time, armed with a list, she bought vegetables and fruit, meat and more bread, cheese and milk, enough for several days. She bought an English newspaper too and a cheap little radio as well as a couple of paperbacks. Thus armed with the rudiments of comfort, she hurried back to plunge once more into the afternoon's duties.

She slipped surprisingly easily into her new job. There were small difficulties with the language, of course, but, save for the cleaners, everyone else spoke English and by the end of the first week, armed with a dictionary and a book of phrases, she managed very well at the shops.

In the canteen she began to make acquaintances among the nursing staff and the young doctors and students and at the end of the second week, bidden to go to the directrice's office, she was informed by that lady that she had proved herself satisfactory and it had been decided that she should remain for a further two weeks. 'This will give you the opportunity to learn a little of our language,' she was told kindly, 'and make some friends.'

Thus encouraged, she embarked on sightseeing. Her next free day was on a Sunday; what better day to view the town, its churches and old buildings? With a bundle of leaflets and a town plan in her hand, Beatrice set off soon after breakfast. The Rapenburg led to Breestraat and she turned away from it to Sint Pieterskerk. The morning service hadn't begun and she spent a little time admiring its vastness before retracing her steps and entering Breestraat again. There was plenty to see here: some delightful sixteenth-century almshouses, another church—fourteenth-century—and then the mound of the Burcht fortification and a covered bridge, before going back to study the façade of the town hall. She stopped for coffee then, before walking along the Oude Singel and then going to peer in the shop windows. Antiques shops abounded; she would find leisure to visit them, she promised herself, and take time to have a good look at some of the small smart boutiques. It was time for lunch by then; she walked back to the Pannekoekenhuis and ate a gigantic pancake filled with crisp bits of bacon and served with syrup. It seemed a strange combination but she was in the mood to try anything once. It was delicious. She drank a pot of coffee and went out into the grey afternoon.

All the museums were open until five o'clock. She went back to the Oude Singel, to the Lakenhal, and spent two pleasant hours looking at furniture, the history of the pilgrim fathers and last of all the paintings—Steen and Rembrandt and Lucas van Leyden. A lovely day, she decided as she went back to the hospital, and she hadn't been lonely, not once. The thought that it would have been nice to have had Professor van der Eekerk there to explain things to her crept into her head but she dismissed it at once as nonsense.

Her sitting-room was warm and cosy and welcoming when she opened her door. There was no denying the fact that it was a good deal more comfortable than her own little place at St Justin's. She made tea and sat reading until it was time to get her supper. The kitchenette was quite perfect; it had everything she could possibly need in it and she cooked her supper with care, set the small table nicely and ate to the strains of music from the radio. Her meal finished, she found her tourist guide and studied it carefully; she would be free on Saturday—perhaps it might be a good idea to visit one of the neighbouring towns...

There were two seminars scheduled for the following week, one in the medical school, the second in the lecture hall of the laboratory block. She was responsible for both of them, arranging the seating and food, making sure that everything was provided for the medical men's comfort. The first went well; she had plenty of help and it was very like a similar meeting at her own hospital. She had allowed herself to wonder if the professor would be there but there was no sign of him. She told herself that she hadn't expected to see him anyway, saw that everything was put to rights and turned her attention to the second seminar.

It was to last for two days and would be attended by a number of eminent specialists from all over Europe; she was anxious that everything should be as perfect as possible, as there would be a variety of tastes to cater for and she only hoped that there would be no language difficulties—Dutch was bad enough, although she had to admit that she had encountered very little trouble so far. The cleaners and domestic staff spoke very little English and understood even less, and her Dutch, confined to a handful of useful phrases, was even poorer, and yet they contrived to understand each other.

The seminar was to start at half-past eight in the morning and she was up early, making a last-minute check and, satisfied that no more could be done for those who would be attending, she went along to the kitchen, had a last word with the staff there and went to stand in the entrance to the lecture hall, ready to smooth the path of anyone who might need help.

There was plenty of time; no one was likely to arrive for another ten minutes, she sat down on a convenient chair and slid her feet out of her neat black shoes.

She didn't hear the quiet footsteps behind her, partly because she wasn't expecting them, nor Professor van der Eekerk's gentle, 'Good morning, Beatrice. Feet hurting? Dear, dear, and the day hardly started!'

She rose to her splendid height. She had been taken by surprise but she refused to be disconcerted, indeed, she didn't feel that at all, she felt delight at the sight of him although she wasn't going to tell him that. Her good morning was civil if uttered in a voice slightly higher than usual. 'There is nothing wrong with my feet, thank you, but since I shall be on them all day I'm giving them a rest while I can.'

He took off his overcoat and threw it on the small counter where presently she would take the coats and hang them up on the rows of pegs behind it.

'Settling in?' he wanted to know. 'I must say you look the part, very prim and professional.'

'Thank you. Where have you been?'

He lifted an eyebrow and she went pink. She said tartly, 'Well, I'm—making conversation.'

'Of course. In Chicago. I got back last night.'

'You must be tired.' She had got her shoes back on, feeling shy for no reason at all. 'Are you reading a paper?'

'Something like that. When are you free, Beatrice?'

'Me, free? Oh, on Saturday—one week it's Saturday and one week Sunday.'

'Good. I'll pick you up at nine o'clock—we'll have a day out.'

'I thought I'd go shopping...'

He said quietly, 'Would you like to spend the day with me, Beatrice?'

She looked at him then, meeting his gaze squarely. 'Yes, please.'

He smiled then and as the sound of voices drew nearer he bent and kissed her.

The hospital director, coming in with the first of the audience, paused at the entrance and thought what an extremely pretty girl Miss Crawley was and such a splendid colour—the wholesome Dutch air must be doing her good. He shook hands with the professor and then turned away to speak to the steady stream of men coming in, while the professor and the other man went into the lecture hall.

Beatrice, kept busy for the next half-hour or so, and then, once the seminar had opened, even busier in the kitchens making sure everything was ready for the coffee and biscuits to be offered when the first paper had been read, was careful not to let her thoughts stray, although she did reflect briefly on his kiss. She had enjoyed it but she mustn't let it turn her head. She was twenty-eight, she reminded herself, with a sensible head on her shoulders.

She didn't see him to speak to again that day. The last paper was read at four o'clock and everyone had gone save a handful of laboratory assistants, hard on the heels of herself and the domestic staff cleaning the place up. There was to be a lecture on forensic medicine in the morning and they were already arranging diagrams and charts on the walls, setting up microscopes, word processors and rows of pipettes and vials. The lecture would last until the coffee-break, there would be a discussion period before lunch and in the afternoon a final paper, given, she knew, by the professor, before everyone would go home and she and her helpers would begin the task of clearing up as quickly as possible, thankful that it was the weekend.

Back in her sitting-room, Beatrice inspected the contents of the fridge and her store cupboard; she would have to eat on Sunday and she had intended to stock up on Saturday before setting out for an afternoon in den Haag.

The professor would have to stop somewhere so that she could buy her Sunday dinner. That problem solved, she turned to the more important one—what to wear. She had not spoken to him at all, only exchanged a brief smile over the heads of those around him. She had no idea what his idea of a day out might be. It was still very cold and there had been a few snowflakes during the afternoon, so she decided on a plain jersey dress in hyacinth-blue with a soft suede belt and her winter coat. Shoes were a problem; if they were to go walking she would need to wear something sensible but supposing they were to go to a restaurant...? She settled on a pair of low-heeled leather shoes which would fit either situation. A velvet beret to match the dress and handbag and gloves completed the outfit, which she hoped would take her through the day.

He knocked on her door at exactly nine o'clock, bade her a cheerful good morning, advised her to find a woolly scarf if she had one, and led her downstairs.

It had been snowing during the night, a thin powder, very white against the dull grey sky. 'Bad weather coming,' commented the professor casually, and opened the car door for her.

Beyond wishing him good morning, Beatrice had said almost nothing, but now she said, 'I thought discussing the weather was an English prerogative?'

He stared down at her. 'We have a great deal to talk about; I thought it best to get the social chit-chat out of the way first.'

She couldn't think of an answer to that; she got into the car and almost fell out again as a large black hairy face with a great many teeth loomed over the seat.

'Fred.' The professor gave her a gentle shove back into her seat. 'As mild as milk. He's delighted to see you.'

Anything less like milk she had yet to see, thought Beatrice, and settled cautiously as he got in beside her. 'What kind of a dog is he?' she wanted to know, and offered a fist to the beast, praying it wouldn't be taken off at the wrist.

It was gently licked and a pair of small yellow eyes twinkled at her through the lavish eyebrows. 'He's rather sweet,' she said. 'Hello, Fred.'

The professor was sitting quietly, making no move to drive away. She turned to look at him. 'Where are we going?' she asked.

'To my home, to meet Alicia and see if you like my house.'

'Is it far?'

'No, no. Ten miles or so. In the country between Leiden and Alphen-aan-de-Rijn—a very small village called Aarledijk.'

They left Leiden and presently the main road to take a country road of bricks, raised above the narrow canals on either side of it. The fields were empty, covered in snow, the flatness broken by clumps of bare trees and farm houses, standing well back from the road. It turned sharply presently, leaving the narrow canals, but now there was a wider waterway beside it, its water thinly iced over, and ahead of them more trees. The professor slowed the car as the road turned into them, shutting off the surrounding fields, but presently the trees thinned and Beatrice could see a church steeple and houses ahead of her. A minute later on the road ended in a cobbled square surrounded by small houses, a shop and the church and, taking up almost all of one side of it, a solid square house behind tall iron railings, its gates wide open.

Beatrice peered out of her window. 'You live here? This is your home?'

He turned to smile at her. 'What did you expect, Beatrice?'

'I don't know—it's old—it looks as though it's been here for ever.'

'Not quite for ever—mostly eighteenth-century and quite a lot older at the back. You shall see for yourself.'

He got out, opened her door, and allowed Fred to get out too, waiting patiently while Beatrice stood on the gravelled sweep before the great front door, taking a look at the portico, the rows of wide windows and the shuttered dormers high up in its steep roof. She turned a glowing face to his. 'It's lovely...'

He didn't say anything, only smiled faintly and urged her gently to the double stone steps and up to the door, Fred padding behind them.

The heavy double door opened as they reached it and a brisk youngish man stood back to allow them to enter.

'Ah, Bilder...' the professor spoke in his own language and then added, 'Beatrice, this is Bilder, who looks after us all. His wife is our cook.'

She put out a hand and Bilder shook it with a polite little bow. He made a short speech in English too which delighted her—Dutch was still something of a mystery to her.

He took her coat and bore it away with his master's and the professor led her across the wide hall to a pair of doors—mahogany with ornate plasterwork about them and, with Fred still at their heels, opened them.

The room was large and by reason of the big windows and high ceiling very light. The walls were covered with a paper, its russet and green dim with age, and the ceiling held a crystal chandelier which reflected the light from the windows and the fire burning in the wide marble fireplace. The carpet was the same russet, its pattern worn thin but still beautiful. There were pictures on the walls and two bow-fronted cabinets each side of the fireplace, facing which was an enormous sofa, flanked by easy-chairs. There was a drum table between the windows and more chairs and everywhere flowers. Beatrice took it all in with one slow scrutiny. 'It's beautiful.'

'Sit down, Beatrice. Bilder is bringing coffee and Alicia will be here in a moment.'

The door opened as he spoke and a child came darting through to fling herself at her father with shouts of delight. He picked her up and hugged her. 'I promised you that I would bring Beatrice—here she is, darling.'

The little girl was like her father; the same blue eyes and regular features and lint-fair hair with an Alice-band and a friendly smile.

Beatrice took the small hand in hers. 'Alicia—I do hope that you speak English, for I can't speak a word of Dutch.'

Her, 'how do you do?' was nicely said and she added with a giggle, 'But Dutch is easy—you must learn it quickly. And may I call you Beatrice?'

'I should like that.'

Alicia had sat down near her and when Bilder brought in the coffee two cats came in with him and went at once to her. 'These are mine,' she told Beatrice, 'Chouchou and Mouser.'

The cats were sleek and nicely plump and looked as though their pedigrees were lacking: Mouser suited his name; a black and white cat with a torn ear and one eye, and Chouchou, a tabby, had only half a tail.

The professor, sitting opposite them, explained, 'They look disreputable but they are Alicia's devoted friends. Fred loves them too.'

Fred, lying in a heap by his master's chair, opened an eye and, as if to demonstrate his affectionate nature, got up and lay down before the fire where the cats joined him.

Beatrice, invited to pour their coffee, reflected that this was a side of the professor about which she knew nothing—something which was to be remedied. She was taken on a tour of the house presently, wandering from room to room and liking them all. Alicia danced along beside her, holding her hand, pointing out anything she particularly wanted Beatrice to admire while the professor contented himself with opening and shutting doors and giving a brief history of each room.

Over lunch Alicia said, 'You haven't seen the attics, Beatrice. There are many. Sometimes Papa takes me up there and we look at things. You must go also, next time you come.'

'They sound great fun, but I shall be going back to England, you know.'

She looked up as she spoke and saw him watching her, a look on his face she couldn't read. More to reassure herself than anything else, she added, 'Quite soon.'

'We would like you to come again, Beatrice, perhaps next Sunday?'

Alicia gave her no choice but to agree vaguely. In any case she very much wanted to. She wanted to know more about Gijs van der Eekerk, and perhaps this would be her only opportunity.

CHAPTER FIVE

AFTER lunch they wrapped up against the cold and went outside so that Beatrice might be shown the grounds at the back of the house, the walled kitchen garden and the field beyond which stretched as far as the canal. 'I have a pony,' said Alicia as she danced along between the two of them, 'and Papa has a big horse. Do you have a horse, Beatrice?'

'No, he wouldn't be very happy in London, would he? But I borrow a friend's horse when I go home.'

'We can all go riding together,' said Alicia happily. A remark it seemed unkind to contradict.

'Where do you stable them?' she asked the professor.

'Beyond the kitchen garden—there's a door at the far end. We have a donkey too; we'll see them next if you like.'

The three beasts were admired, given sugar and carrots and patted lovingly by Alicia. The donkey was old and meek.

'Have you had him a long time?'

'Just over a year—we bought him from a passing traveller.'

'Papa was angry with the man, he was beating Flossy and hurting her and he didn't want her any more, but we did, didn't we, Papa?'

'She's company for the other two. Shall we go in and see what's for tea?'

After a tea she hadn't expected—scones and fairy-cakes and a big Dundee cake and tea leaves in the teapot not teabags—Beatrice was taken upstairs again to meet Nanny, who had been to spend her Sunday with a friend in Leiden. She was a Scotswoman, elderly, with a placid face framed by iron-grey hair, and Beatrice had the distinct impression that she herself was being summed up by the shrewd grey eyes.

'You're a bonny girl,' observed Nanny finally. 'I do like a woman to be a woman, if you get my meaning—I have no liking for these wafer-thin girls with their skirts too short and their mussed up hair.'

'Well,' said Beatrice mildly, 'I'm a bit old for that, you know.'

The professor and his small daughter were bending over a puzzle on the playroom table. 'But you have very nice legs,' he said.

Presently Alicia was led away to bed. She lifted her face for a kiss as she wished Beatrice goodnight. 'You *will* come again next week—Papa says so.'

When Beatrice hesitated she said anxiously, 'Papa, Beatrice must come—you must ask her again...'

The professor stood before his hearth, his hands in his trouser pockets; he looked exactly what he was, reflected Beatrice, a man of an old family living in an old house, self-assured, handsome and sure of what he wanted from life.

'I hope—we both hope that you will spend as much time with us as possible, Beatrice.'

When she didn't reply he added, 'If you would like that.'

He wasn't going to accept a vague non-committal reply, the kind of answer one would give, not meaning a word of it, at some social gathering.

'Yes, I would like that, thank you for asking me.'

He smiled then. 'Good, now you may sleep happily, Alicia.'

The child hugged him, took long-drawn-out farewells of the cats and Fred, reminded them that they were to tuck her up presently, and went upstairs with Nanny.

The professor took a pocket watch from his waistcoat and glanced at it before coming to sit in a wing chair opposite Beatrice. 'At least fifteen minutes before Alicia is in bed...'

'Then I think I should go back.'

'You are going out this evening?' The question sounded casual.

'Me? No...'

'You will return and cook yourself a meal and eat it alone with a book propped up against the pepperpot.'

She laughed. 'Well, yes, but it's not as bad as it sounds. I'm used to being by myself when I'm off duty.' She sounded matter-of-fact.

'However this evening you will dine with me, I hope, and afterwards I will drive you back whenever you wish. I shall be home for the next week or two. I have work here at the hospital as well as in Amsterdam and Utrecht—they're both near enough for me to come home each evening.'

'That's nice for Alicia. She's a dear little girl—and happy.'

'I hope so. She needs a mother.'

A remark which reminded her that he was intending to marry shortly. Watching her expressive face, the professor smiled to himself.

She sought for something to say. 'It'll be nice for you too.'

'Very nice,' he agreed smoothly.

She bent to stroke Mouser's bullet head, glad to have something to do in a silence that had become rather too long.

'I think we might go upstairs,' suggested her host, and she went with him, up the beautiful staircase to the smaller gallery above and along the short passage which led to Alicia's room. She was in bed, sitting up against her pillow, rosy from her bath while Nanny put her clothes ready for the morning. The professor sat down on the edge of her bed and after a moment Beatrice did the same on the other side.

'You will come again soon?' begged the child.

'Yes, I promise, love, but don't forget that I'll be going back to England soon; perhaps later on you can come and visit me there?'

'At your home?'

'Yes, it's in the country.'

Alicia nodded. 'Papa will arrange that.'

Oh, dear, thought Beatrice, I shouldn't have said that. She had meant it to be a gentle reminder that she would be going back to England and they weren't likely to meet again, but the child had taken her at her word. It was made worse by his cheerful, 'Why not? Don't let me forget, *liefje*.'

Downstairs again, he poured her a drink and went to sit opposite her again, a glass of whisky on the tulipwood tripod table by his chair. He made no mention of her return to England and she sought a way to tell him that she had spoken to Alicia on the spur of the moment but she was given no chance. He took the conversation into his own hands, rambling on pleasantly from one impersonal topic to the next until Bilder came to tell them that dinner was served.

Beatrice, sitting in the splendour of the dining-room, made polite replies to his gentle remarks. The situation, she felt, was getting out of hand; she had promised to return to his home, she had suggested that Alicia should visit her in England and the child had believed her to be sincere. Also she had never intended to stay for so long.

Gijs, sitting back in his chair, watching her, aware of her thoughts, smiled again. He said casually, 'I dare say that you are tired in the evenings when you have gone off duty. Do you have a chance to go out during the day?'

'During the lunch-hour—the shops are close by...' She remembered suddenly that she hadn't bought any food—there was bread, butter and some eggs and cheese—it would have to be an omelette.

'You have remembered something which you ought to have done?'

They were back in the drawing-room drinking their coffee. 'Well, yes, but it doesn't matter—just some shopping.' She added cheerfully, 'It doesn't matter in the least; there's plenty in the fridge.'

She thought of the asparagus, the salmon *en croute* and the peach pavlova she had just eaten; it wouldn't hurt her to eat sparingly after all that richness.

Bilder came into the room to take the coffee-tray and the professor spoke to him, giving him instructions, she supposed, and gave a quick glance at the long-case clock in the corner of the room.

'Let us sit here for a little longer,' suggested Gijs. 'Tell me, Beatrice, what do you think of Holland? I know that you have seen nothing of it, but it must have made some impression—even such a short time in Leiden?'

'I feel at home here. Leiden is old and...' she sought for a word '...settled in centuries of living. So are a great many other towns, but somehow I feel happy here; it doesn't seem foreign at all.'

She looked around at the lovely room. 'And this beautiful house. You must be happy here.

My home is rather nice, I think, but as you know it's quite different.' It might be as well to change the subject; she went on, 'The hospital here is a splendid one, isn't it? The research centre and path. labs are very much better than St Justin's, although I suppose I shouldn't say that.'

'Had you ever thought of leaving?'

'Often—the East End of London isn't ideal, is it? But it's quite hard to get work, you know.'

'Do you need to work? You don't, do you?'

'No, but I couldn't live in idleness at home.'

'You could marry—you must have had several chances to do that.'

'Well, yes, but somehow none of them was right...'

His voice was quiet. 'And what is right?'

'I'm not sure. Being friends and liking the same things and wanting to do things together. Being in love is fine but it isn't enough, is it?'

'No—and I know what you mean.' His voice was impersonal as he went on, 'I thought that it was enough when I married Zalia. One needs to love as well as be in love. We discovered very soon that was true. She was very young and pretty and she hadn't wanted Alicia. She left us when Alicia was almost a year old. She was killed in a car accident in Italy. She had been living there with an American.'

'I'm so sorry. How dreadful for you and for Alicia. Does she remember anything of her mother? She was too young, surely...'

'Nothing at all.'

'I am glad that you are going to marry again; you must be lonely.'

She wished that he would talk about his future wife and wondered uneasily if she might object to Beatrice being at the professor's house even though it had been to please Alicia. When he didn't answer she flushed a little; he would think that she was prying...she made haste to plunge into a harmless topic, the first one she could think of, the weather.

'Do you think it will snow?'

He gave a snort of laughter.

'What's so funny about that question?' asked Beatrice sharply.

'I am reminded of when we met...'

'Oh, I remember very clearly; you said what a pity it was that we couldn't say what we wished to.' She studied his face. 'But that doesn't always do, you know—and the weather's safe.'

He smiled then. 'And you wish to be safe, do you not, my dear?' He stirred Fred's head with the toe of his shoe. 'I go too fast.'

She said crossly, 'I don't know what you're talking about. I think that I should go back now.'

He got to his feet at once, and if she felt a twinge of regret that he hadn't begged her to stay a little longer she didn't allow it to be there for more than a second.

It was dark and very cold outside. Gijs drove back almost without speaking and when he stopped at the institute door he told her to wait. He got out himself with the faithful Fred in close attendance and went round to the boot, to return to open her door, holding a box under one arm.

He ignored her carefully rehearsed thank-you speech but took her arm and urged her inside the building. The three of them went up the stairs to her little flat where he unlocked the door, switched on the lights and put the box down upon the table.

The room was warm but as impersonal as an hotel room and after the lovely surroundings in which she had spent her day it seemed less than welcoming.

Gijs drew the curtains. 'Is this place empty?' he wanted to know.

'I expect so—the path. labs work on Saturdays and Sundays but only until four o'clock.'

He nodded. 'Don't open the door to anyone, Beatrice. Is the door below locked at night?'

'Oh, yes. One of the porters comes over when the last technician has gone.'

He went to the phone and spoke to someone at the other end and when she looked questioningly at him said, 'I've told the head porter to send someone over to lock up in five minutes' time.'

'I'm not in the least nervous.'

'If I thought that I would stay.' At her look of astonishment he added, 'When I am gone, clear your pretty head of the weather and think about today.' He was standing close to her and bent and kissed her cheek and was gone before she could utter.

'Well, really,' said Beatrice, and put a hand to her cheek. Her eye fell on the box he had left on the table and she went to open it.

Inside, beautifully packed, were several dishes; slices of cold chicken, a winter salad, soup in a covered container, a chocolate mousse, croissants and butter, crisp little biscuits tipped with chocolate and, tucked down the side, a half-bottle of hock. 'Well, really,' said Beatrice again, but this time her voice held delight.

Two of the path. labs were in use the next day and one of the research professors came in for a few hours. She attended to their various wants, cleared up when they had gone, got ready for the morning and went back to her flat. She hadn't been there for five minutes before the phone rang.

'You have had a busy day?' enquired the professor.

'No, no. Hardly anything to do, just to be here in case I was needed. I'm glad you rang. Thank you for the box of goodies. I shall have a lovely supper presently. How very kind you are.'

His grunt could have meant anything. 'I shall call for you tomorrow evening at half-past seven,' he told her. 'We will dine in Leidschendam—that's a few miles to the south of Leiden. Goodnight, Beatrice.'

He rang off and she put the phone down. 'I might not want to go,' she muttered. 'He just takes it for granted that I want to see him again.'

She fell silent, because that was exactly what she did want.

The morning was busy; she ate a quick lunch in the canteen, fetched her outdoor things and hurried out for half an hour. The Bentley was parked in the forecourt and she hurried past and out into Rapenburg, anxious, for some reason, not to come face to face with Gijs.

He watched her go, standing at a window, waiting to teach a class of students. Snow was beginning to fall in soft lazy flurries, making it impossible to see her. He turned away and made his way to the class waiting for him.

It was still snowing when he came for her that evening and she was standing in her stockinged feet trying to decide whether to wear a pair of sensible black pumps or the frivolous sandals. She was wearing the blue velvet dress again; he would probably think that she had nothing else but she didn't care about that. It was warm, and besides it flattered her smooth creamy skin. She opened the door to him, the shoes still in her hand and he said at once, 'Oh, the plain slippers—just supposing we hit a snowdrift and have to walk!' He kissed her with the air of a man who had got into the habit of it, light and quick against her cheek, and she told herself that it was the thought of the evening ahead which sent her heart racing.

Careful, she admonished herself as she put on her shoes, don't get involved—he's as good as married. He helped her into her coat and locked the door after them and when they got downstairs she found that he had driven the Bentley to within a foot or so of the door. 'Wait,' he told her and opened the car door, picked her up and tossed her on to the seat and closed the door on her gasp.

Getting in beside her, he observed, 'I hope you're hungry. I seem to have missed lunch...'

'You were at the hospital?' She added quickly, 'That's a silly thing to say, I saw the car when I went out.'

'I watched you from a window. Were you afraid that you would meet me? You had the appearance of someone making a stealthy getaway.'

She laughed. 'Not afraid...'

'Good.' He was driving out of town, taking an inner road through Voorschoten and presently reached Leidschendam and the restaurant. It was an elegant place and, despite the weather, almost full. Beatrice was glad of the blue velvet and at the same time regretted the sandals. Still, the dress was long and the black slippers were elegant even if on the plain side.

They had a corner table, its pink-shaded lamp casting a becoming glow over her face.

She looked across at him and smiled. 'This is nice. Do you come here often?'

His faint smile and lifted eyebrow brought colour to her cheeks. 'I'm not being nosy,' she said with a snap, 'just making conversation.'

'I had hoped we had overcome that stumbling-block—making conversation. We have a great deal to say to each other.'

The *maître d'* came then and they discussed the menu in a leisurely manner. 'Champagne, don't you think?' He did not wait for her to answer but lifted a finger for the wine waiter. Only when he had gone and they sat, she with her sherry, he with his genever, did he continue with what he had been saying. 'There is a good deal to discuss.'

'What?'

'Us—our future.' He uttered the words in an unhurried, placid voice.

'I don't understand...'

'That is why we have to talk.'

She stared down at the plate before her, speared a morsel of mushroom nestling succulently in its bed of madeira sauce and garlic and popped it into her mouth. When she looked up at him he was smiling. 'Will you marry me, Beatrice?'

She swallowed the mushroom without tasting it.

He went on smoothly. 'Oh, not immediately. You will need time to get used to the idea, give in your notice, talk it over with your family...'

'Why on earth do you want to marry me?' she asked in a sudden rush. 'We don't even know each other well, besides I don't—that is, you don't...'

She went rather pink although she met his eyes squarely.

'You seek romance? Naturally, I suppose all women do. But where has it got you? A man like Tom, eating all the sandwiches while he keeps a close eye on his prospects under cover of lifelong devotion. I'll share my sandwiches, Beatrice, and I have no need of prospects, nor will I pretend lifelong devotion, only a sincere liking, an abiding friendship and a promise to care for your happiness.'

'But you don't...' she began and he finished for her.

'Love you? Neither of us has had much success with love, have we?'

She remembered something. 'But you said you intended to marry.'

'So I did. You.'

She ate some more mushrooms because she couldn't think of anything to say and, apparently not minding this, the professor finished his and sat back in his chair. He expected her to say something, she supposed; after all a girl had to answer when she had a proposal. The waiter took their plates and served their fish with a delicate sauce and baby new potatoes. She took a sip of champagne. 'You don't expect me to answer now, do you?'

'Certainly not. Think about it, get used to the idea if you will; when you get back to St Justin's we can arrange for you to leave. In the meantime let us continue to get to know each other a little more. You have your doubts, but I am sure that we shall suit each other very well.'

'Alicia—she might be made unhappy.'

'On the contrary, she wishes you to be her mama; I hear from Nanny that she is planning her bridesmaid's dress.'

Beatrice caught at her last remnants of good sense. 'It's all so sudden.' Exactly the kind of remark a shrinking Victorian miss would have made, she thought crossly.

'No, it is not. Two people meet and know at once that they share something: liking, hating, loving. They may not be aware of it but all the same they have known subconsciously. Sooner or later they will realise it.'

He spoke in a matter-of-fact manner, smiling at her kindly across the table. She said slowly, 'I'll think about it.'

'Good girl. I'll come for you tomorrow evening and take you home to see Alicia. Now what would you like for dessert? The *bavaroise* is good.' He began to talk about other things, never mentioning his proposal again, only as he wished her goodnight at her door did he remind her to be ready on the following evening and this time his kiss left her light-headed.

'I've had too much champagne,' she told herself, locking the door after him. 'I'll think sensibly in the morning.'

Certainly she thought about him in the morning but not as sensibly as she had intended, but during the day she had made up her mind to make some excuse when he came for her that evening—a headache, an unexpected phone call from home, her hair to be washed. Her good resolutions were flung to the wind a few minutes before he had said he would call for her; Tom telephoned.

'Have you missed me?' he wanted to know. He didn't wait for an answer. 'We'll have an evening out as soon as you get back.' And when she began to protest he said, 'Don't worry, darling, I've quite forgotten your little outbursts; be sure I'll be on the look-out for you when you get back.'

She hung up before he could say anything else just as she heard the doorbell.

If the professor was surprised at the eager welcome she gave him he gave no sign. He closed the door behind him and wandered into the room. 'What has upset you, or should I say who?'

He flung an arm round her shoulders and she felt instantly better.

'Tom phoned, just a few minutes ago.'

'Still in love with you, is he?' The professor's voice was sympathetic and at the same time brisk.

'No—at least he didn't say so, only that he missed me and he said he'd quite forgotten all the things I had said and he'd be on the look-out for me when I got back.'

'And...?'

'I hung up on him.'

He laughed gently. 'Yes, I would imagine that you did. We must think of a way of discouraging him, mustn't we?'

'How?'

'We can discuss that later. Now we will forget the man and go home and tuck Alicia up in her bed and then have dinner together. I've had a busy day—it will be nice to talk to someone about it.'

She got her coat and went down to the car with him and presently he drove away, out of the forecourt, into Rapenburg and away from Leiden.

The night was freezing, the snow stiff with frost, a cold moon turning it to silver. Beatrice tucked her chin into her coat collar and relished the warmth, faintly redolent of leather, seeping into her bones.

'Is it always as cold as this?' she wanted to know.

'It varies. Weather like this may last for several weeks, but usually much less than that. One more day and skating will be allowed. The ice has to be of a sufficient depth before the children are allowed on to it.'

'You skate?'

He sounded surprised. 'Of course.' He glanced at her. 'You will learn quickly enough.'

'I shan't be here for long enough...'

'There will be other winters.'

They were on the narrow road leading to the village, surrounded by a flat white world. 'I haven't——' she began. 'That is, I've been too busy to think. I'm sure it wouldn't work.'

'How can you know if you haven't considered it carefully?' He added placidly, 'But perhaps it is a good idea if you wait until you are back at St Justin's and have seen Tom.'

'You said that to annoy me,' said Beatrice tartly. 'You know very well that I don't want anything more to do with him.'

'You are bound to meet him from time to time. A man in love will always find a way to see the girl he has lost his heart to.' He slowed the Bentley as they entered the village. 'Are you just a little afraid of meeting him again, Beatrice?'

'Not afraid, just... well, how can I make him see?'

He had stopped in front of his door. 'Don't worry about that, just leave it to me.' He got out and opened her door and they went into the house.

Alicia was waiting for them, ready for bed in a pink woolly dressing-gown and furry slippers, Fred was there too and Chouchou and Mouser, neither of whom did more than lift their heads before going back to sleep before the drawing-room fire.

The little girl was hugged and kissed, talking all the time to both her father and Beatrice and finally, their coats taken from them and sitting by the fire, with her between them on a stool and Fred lying over his master's feet, the professor observed, 'It's long past your bedtime, *liefje*.'

'Five minutes, Papa. I must just tell Beatrice something most special.'

'What's that, love?' asked Beatrice.

'My dress,' said Alicia breathlessly, 'pink and long and I must have pink slippers and a wreath in my hair.' She frowned. 'You haven't forgotten that you are to marry Papa?'

Beatrice said slowly, 'No, I hadn't forgotten, but I haven't quite decided.'

'He will be a splendid husband,' piped Alicia, 'I heard Mevrouw Bilder tell Nanny...'

Beatrice cast a cold look at the professor. 'I seem to be the only one——' she began icily.

'Well, of course—you must understand that everyone else has made up their minds that we are to marry, but that need not influence you in any way. You are free to make your own choice, Beatrice. I'll not stand in your way if you find that Tom's devotion is too deep to resist.'

He smiled at her kindly and his deep voice was full of conviction, but the suspicion that he was amused made her frown. 'I'm sure I don't know,' she said peevishly.

'You like that I wear a pink dress?' asked Alicia uncertainly.

Beatrice's heart smote her, Alicia's small face looked unhappy.

'I think you'll look lovely in pink,' she said, 'just like a princess.'

'So, having got that knotty point settled, how about bed?' Her father lifted her off the stool and carried her to the door just as Nanny came into the hall.

'I've not said goodnight to Beatrice,' objected the moppet.

Beatrice nipped across the room to be embraced and to kiss a warm cheek. 'Tomorrow?' asked Alicia.

'I have to go to Brussels tomorrow,' the professor told her, 'but I'm sure Nanny will let you telephone to Beatrice before you go to bed.'

Beatrice felt a pang of disappointment which she squashed at once. Just because Gijs had taken her out once or twice was no reason to suppose that she would miss him. That he had asked her to marry him was something which she disregarded completely. It was quite impossible, she told herself. Liking wasn't enough; on the other hand to fall in love and marry without thought of the everyday aspect of marriage—the friendship, the similar likes and dislikes, the pleasure of each other's company, the wish to be together—that would be disastrous.

'I shall be back in three days' time,' said Gijs placidly.

To her secret annoyance, he said not a word about his proposal; indeed by the end of the evening she wondered if she had dreamt the whole thing. He was amusing, thoughtful for her comfort, the perfect host, keeping up a casual conversation which nonetheless touched on neither of them.

He took her back later that evening, saw her to her flat and bade her goodbye, dropping a casual kiss on her cheek as he did so.

'May I call for you in three days' time— some time after seven o'clock?'

He didn't wait for an answer.

She told herself that it was all nonsense that she should miss him, but she did. She went out each evening with Hetty and some of the nurses and on one afternoon when she was free she accepted an invitation to visit a museum with one of the house doctors she had met in the canteen. He was an earnest young man, intent on showing her as much as possible, but since the museum he had chosen was the National Science Museum and she knew almost nothing about cartography, astronomy or chemistry, she went back to the hospital with a headache and strong longing for a cup of tea.

As luck would have it, one of the cleaners went off sick during the last afternoon so that Beatrice had to take over her work as well as her own. It was well after six o'clock by the time she got to her flat and she tore out of her clothes and under the shower and then dressed in a plain jersey two-piece in a warm copper colour. She had just finished doing her hair to her satisfaction when the bell rang and she went to open the door.

'I missed you,' observed the professor. He brushed her cheek, shed his overcoat and followed her into the little sitting-room.

Beatrice felt a warm glow of delight at the sight of him. If it had been Tom, she reflected, he would have asked her if she had missed him...

She asked, 'Have you been busy?'

'Yes. It is no weather for driving either.'

'You took the car to Brussels?'

'I drive whenever I possibly can.' He was wandering around the room, looking at the few pictures on its walls. 'Did you know that you are to go back to St Justin's in a couple of days' time?'

She sat up at that. 'No. Are you sure? No
one has said anything to me.'

'I'm sure—I'm on the hospital committee.
He looked at her over his shoulder. 'You have
been entirely satisfactory but now it is the turn
of someone from Edinburgh. Juffrouw
Winkelhuisen is to go to Cologne. The devil
of it is that I have to go to Groningen, to the
medical school—I've some examining to do
there—so I won't be able to see you away.'

'What a pity.' She hoped her voice sounded
sufficiently casual, 'But I'm sure I can
manage—I shall meet the others at the
airport.'

'Supposing Tom is waiting for you?' He
frowned. 'I don't like the idea of him bothering you.' He came to stand in front of her.
'Have you decided to marry me, Beatrice?'

She looked up at him and saw nothing but
kindness and concern in his face. She said, 'I
have missed you . . .'

'Very much?' She nodded.

'Go back to St Justin's. I think that perhaps
when you are there you will know. I want you
to do something for me.' He took something
from his pocket. 'Wear this; perhaps it will
make Tom realise that you meant what you
said. There are no strings attached, Beatrice;
it is, after all, only a ring.'

He held out his hand and showed her what ay in his palm. A gold ring. 'It has been in ny family for a very long time—a poesy ring.'

She took it from him and studied it. There's something written—it's almost worn hrough.'

'"*A vous et nul autre*". You and no other— t is a seventeenth-century wedding-ring.' He ook her hand and slipped the ring on her finger. 'It fits very well. You will wear it?'

Beatrice looked up into his smiling face. Yes,' she said.

CHAPTER SIX

ALICIA was waiting for them, sitting before the fire with an arm around Fred's neck and Mouser and Chouchou crowded on her small lap. She flew to meet them, scattering the cats, the big dog beside her.

'Papa,' she shrilled, 'Beatrice...I have much to say. I have been good at school and so I do not have to go to bed until I have told you.' She lifted her face for their kisses. 'Just a little while?' she added coaxingly.

'Ten minutes! Come back to the fire and tell us about your day.'

Beatrice, sitting at one end of the great sofa, watched the animated little face, pouring out the day's doings, and thought how pleasant it was sitting there with Mouser on her knee and the warm fire sending a glow over the beautiful room. Just for a moment she was lost in a dream wherein she was indeed sitting there, Gijs's wife and Alicia's stepmother, secure, wrapped around by love, completely content. She thrust the dream aside; she was perfectly secure as she was and who was there to wrap her around with love? Gijs hadn't mentioned it. Liking, compatability, the pleasure of her company, Alicia's fondness for her, all those had been mentioned, but not love. His attitude towards her was that of an affectionate friend. Her own attitude towards him, she wasn't prepared to think about just then. In any case, she was given small chance, for Alicia's voice demanded to know how long it would be before she came back to Holland.

A difficult question, not made any easier by Gijs, sitting in his chair looking annoyingly bland, and not saying a word to help her.

Back in her flat once more with Gijs's cheerful goodbye still ringing in her ears and the touch of his mouth against her cheek still vivid in her mind, Beatrice made no effort to get ready for bed. She sat down, still in her coat, and thought about her evening. It had been delightful; dinner had been delicious, served by the discreet Bilder, she had a little chat with Nanny, who had looked at the poesy ring with a knowing smile although she hadn't actually said anything. All the same, Beatrice knew that she was approved of and that was important. She and Gijs had spent the rest of the evening sitting by the fire once again, sometimes talking, sometimes silent. She imagined that if they were to marry that would be how they would spend their evenings, content with each other's company, with no need to entertain each other.

The professor had talked about his work and she could sense that it was an important part of his life, although he was quite prepared to share it with her. If she ignored the fact that they weren't in love, she felt reasonably certain that they would be happy together.

She went to bed at last, her mind in a fine muddle.

The following morning she was told that she would be going back to St Justin's. The director pronounced himself entirely satisfied with her work, indeed he expressed regret that she wasn't to stay longer. Though, as he pointed out, the scheme, to be successful, entailed making as many exchanges as possible. Her departure would be arranged for her, she need do nothing, but perhaps she would be good enough to show the young woman coming to replace her from Edinburgh exactly what she should do.

'Hetty will be of great help, I know,' said the director, 'but perhaps the young lady will feel more at home if you take her under your wing for a day.'

The days were busy now; Beatrice made sure that the cleaning staff knew that someone would be coming in her place, told those whom she knew that she would be leaving and did some hasty present-buying. Alicia phoned in the evenings but there was no word from Gijs. Beatrice twisted and twiddled the ring on her finger and thought how tiresome he was. The only reason she wore it was because it would make an end, once and for all, of Tom's persistence. She phoned her mother too, fending off that lady's artless questions about the professor, explaining that until she got back to London she had no idea as to when she would be home. Despite all this activity she found the days long and empty...

The last day came with no word from Gijs. She told herself that she hadn't expected to hear from him anyway. She gave a small farewell party that evening so that Hetty and her friends and one or two of the housemen could meet the girl from Edinburgh, a delightful creature with red hair and bright blue eyes and a soft Highland voice. She was very sensible too, making no heavy weather of learning her way around the institute.

When the actual moment of leaving came, Beatrice didn't want to go. It had nothing to do with her job; it meant leaving Leiden and Gijs. She was going to miss his friendship for of course once she was back in England she would tell him that marrying him simply wouldn't do.

She would give him back his ring, for after all it had been a loan just to make things easier with Tom, and thank him for all his kindness... Even now he might be regretting everything he had said to her.

She met the rest of the party from St Justin's at Schiphol and since they had so much news to exchange they were at Heathrow before they realised it. Beatrice listening to Sister Watts' colourful description of the theatre work she had done, looked out of the taxi window and thought how different London was from Leiden. She supposed that she would get used to it again. She twiddled the ring on her gloved hand and wondered if she would ever see Gijs again. She hadn't expected to feel like this, as though she had just lost something that she couldn't do without.

They dispersed in the hospital entrance hall to go to their various rooms. They would be interviewed in due course, in the meantime they were to settle in again. Juffrouw Winkelhuisen was ready to leave; it would be merely a question of handing over keys and any information which she thought necessary.

Half an hour later, Beatrice shut the door on her and started to unpack. Everything was in apple-pie order; as soon as she had made herself a cup of tea she would go round the place and have a word with everyone.

She was interrupted by the doorbell. Surely not Tom, she thought, and if it was she didn't want to see him, not yet anyway. She opened the door on its chain and saw nothing but a wealth of red roses.

'Name of Crawley?' said a reassuringly Cockney voice from behind the bouquet.

'Yes, that's me,' said Beatrice, regardless of grammar. 'Wait a sec.' She rummaged in her purse, opened the door and exchanged the roses for a few coins. 'Thank you.'

''E must luv yer,' commented the youthful messenger, tearing down the stairs. A sentiment Beatrice echoed but with a note of doubt. They might not be from Gijs... However, they were. Two dozen red roses with a card attached. She read it smiling and then read it again, not smiling anymore. 'Pleasant memories and best wishes for the future.' If that wasn't a clear indication that he considered their pleasant interlude just that and nothing else. Never mind the ring, he had done that to make things easier for her if she saw Tom and, as for all that talk about marrying, it had been nothing but an amusing little game for Alicia's benefit. That none of this made sense in the light of past events was something she disregarded. All the same, she arranged the roses in a variety of vases and set them round the room. They made a splendid show.

It was inevitable that she would see Tom the next day on her way back from the hospital after an interview with the hospital manager. It had been an entirely satisfactory interview and she wasn't hurrying back, mulling over the nice things the manager had had to say about her work. He was beside her, an arm possessively on hers before she realised it.

'There you are, darling, I guessed you'd be over here sometime about now. Have you missed me? Our pleasant little evenings together? Get a few days off; we'll go to your parents. I'm sure I can manage a couple of days; heaven knows I've worked hard enough. You have no idea how busy I've been while you've been living at ease.'

Beatrice had come to a halt. 'Tom, let go of my arm. I haven't missed you, I haven't even thought of you and I've no intention of taking you home. What can I say to convince you that I don't want to marry you?'

She remembered the ring then. 'Well, perhaps this will convince you.' She held up her hand with the ring and watched his look of astonishment.

'Good lord, you sly minx, the moment my back's turned...'

'Don't talk nonsense, Tom.' She began to walk away.

'Who is it?' He laughed. 'Or is it a trick to send me packing?'

'No, no, it's no trick. Now I'm going back to my work.'

She left him there and hurried back to work. She had been calm enough with Tom but now she found herself shivering; she wasn't sure if it was fright or rage or exasperation at his refusal to give her up.

There was too much to do to give her time to brood over it; she had lunch in the canteen, the object of a good deal of interest, and went back to her afternoon chores. The path. labs were busier than usual; there was a good deal of coming and going and requests for tea and coffee as well as fresh supplies of pipettes, paper, slides and other oddments and a small crisis to be dealt with halfway through the af-

ternoon when one of the computers malfunc-
tioned and she was called upon to find
someone to see to it without loss of time.

She went to her room finally, intent on an
early night. She would have a shower, get into
her dressing-gown, make herself some supper
and watch television. She had phoned her
mother to tell her that she would be home at
the weekend, but she had promised to phone
Alicia...she would do that as soon as she had
showered.

She had her hand on the receiver when she
heard the doorbell. Tom. She stood still, determined to ignore it but when it pealed for
the third time she went to the door, kept it
on the chain and peered round the opening.
It wasn't Tom. She flung the door wide and
hurled herself at the professor's massive chest.
'Gijs, oh, Gijs, it's you!' Her voice was
muffled by his waistcoat.

'What a delightful welcome.' He put an arm
around her, shut the door and stood leaning
against it. Then said, 'You thought that I was
Tom.'

She nodded without looking at him.

'He's been bothering you?'

'Well, just a bit.' She gave a long sigh. 'I
showed him the ring but he thought I was

making it up.' She sniffed. 'Thank you for the lovely roses.'

He patted the top of her head in a comforting fashion. 'Let us go somewhere quiet and talk,' he suggested in a voice which wasn't going to take no for an answer. He stood her away from him and eyed her thoughtfully. 'You look very nice like that—I like the hair. Go and put some clothes on and we'll be on our way.'

'I was just going to ring Alicia.'

'I'll do that.' He gave her a gentle pat. 'Off you go—no need to dress up.'

She put on the first thing that came to hand and bundled her hair up in a knot in the nape of her neck, a flick of powder and a trace of lipstick and she was ready. She came from behind the curtain and saw that Gijs was by the telephone talking to Alicia. As she crossed the room he said, 'Here she is now, *liefje*. Sleep well.'

He handed Beatrice the phone and wandered away to look out of the windows at the chimney-pots beyond. When she put it down he said, 'You're tired; we don't need to talk unless you want to. Just a quiet hour or two...'

There was nothing she wanted more. She asked, 'What about you? Have you been here all day?'

'I flew over from Groningen a couple of hours ago.' He turned his head to smile at her and she saw then that he was tired, lines she hadn't noticed before etched in his face.

'You're far more tired than I—Gijs, shall I make an omelette or scrambled eggs or something and *you* can have a quiet hour or two? Have you a lecture to give tomorrow?'

'No—I'll have to go back to Leiden in the morning.' He smiled gently. 'I wanted to be sure that you were safely here.'

She stood staring at him, knowing all of a sudden that, never mind the muddle her thoughts were in, of one thing she was sure. She had fallen in love with him, more—she loved him, she wanted to sit him in a chair and fetch his slippers and pour his whisky and sit at his knee and listen to his voice. That he would very much dislike being waited on didn't matter. She went quite pale with the strength of her feelings and then blushed at his lifted eyebrows. 'A penny for them?' he invited.

She shook her head. 'Just—nothing.' She watched his face. 'Well, it was something—something I thought.'

He smiled again. 'Shall we go?'

He drove west through the city and at first Beatrice didn't take much notice of where they were going. Presently, though, she noticed that they had left the busy heart of the city. 'Aren't we near St James's Park?' she wanted to know.

'On your left; Green Park's ahead of us.' He turned the car into a quiet tree-lined street which in turn opened into a small square. The houses here were handsome with stone steps leading to the elegant front doors and more steps leading down to basements. The professor stopped before one of them and opened his door.

'Is this a restaurant?' asked Beatrice as she got out.

'I have a flat here—I come to London so often I need to have a *pied-à-terre*. Toogood will have a meal ready for us.'

Who was Toogood? she wondered as they crossed the narrow pavement and went into the foyer with a porter sitting by the desk. He wished them good evening and the professor said, 'No need for the lift, thank you, Soames,' and urged her up the thickly carpeted staircase to the floor above. There were several doors in the wide corridor; one of them was opened by a youngish man who wished them good evening in a cheerful voice and expressed his pleasure at seeing his master again, returned Beatrice's greeting with suitable dignity, took her coat and opened a door in the small hall.

'Supper in half an hour, sir?' he wanted to know. 'And would Miss Crawley care to step along to the cloakroom?'

There was no point in doing so, she decided; she had dressed in a hurry and she had no doubt that her hair was a mess and her make-up sketchy, an opinion echoed by the professor, who touched her hair lightly and said, 'I don't know why you don't let it hang down your back.'

'That would do very nicely if I were eighteen; you know very well that I'm twenty-eight.'

He laughed, 'Come and sit down. Toogood will tell us when he is ready.'

'Does he look after the flat for you?'

'Yes, he lives here all the time so that when I come over, sometimes unexpectedly, I have somewhere to come to. I brought Alicia here last year and they got on splendidly. He took her to the zoo and Madame Tussaud's while I was working. He's a splendid cook and looks after the place very well. Someone comes in to help him several times a week.'

He got up to offer her a drink, put the glass down on the little pie-crust table by her chair and went back to his own armchair.

'You are wearing the poesy ring. You showed it to Tom?'

'Yes, oh, yes, I did, he called me a sly minx...'

'Dear, oh, dear. You are, I think, just a little afraid of him.'

'Not afraid of him, but I am afraid of the unpleasantness—of having to meet him.'

His next remark took her completely by surprise. 'Have you decided to marry me, Beatrice?'

He would expect her to say what she thought, not nibble round his question with a lot of vague answers, but she would have to be careful not to let him see what her true feelings were.

'Yes, I should like to marry you, Gijs, only it's rather awkward now, isn't it? It looks as though I'm doing it just to escape from Tom.'

'Let me put your mind at rest, Beatrice, I don't think anything of the kind. I hope you will marry me because you like me and because you like Alicia. I believe that we can be very happy together and I suggest that we marry as soon as possible. Time enough to get to know each other better once we are married.'

She was glad that he did not pretend to more than liking, but had he not said when he met her that he had no patience with meaningless talk? And liking was a very good basis for loving.

She looked up as he spoke. 'May I bring Alicia with me at the weekend and visit your parents?'

'Yes, of course—I'll let them know first about us.'

'You will wish to marry here from your home?'

'Yes, please, only isn't it rather awkward for you?'

'Not in the least. We can perhaps, see the rector at the weekend? I'll see about a licence.'

'The banns take three weeks...'

'Banns? Ah, yes, but I'll get a special licence. In that way we can marry as soon as you can be ready.'

She felt like someone on rollerskates who couldn't stop. 'I have to give in my notice here.'

'I'll see about that tomorrow.' He got up out of his chair and went and pulled her to her feet. 'You do believe that we shall be happy together?'

She stared up into his calm face. 'Yes, I do.' She smiled at him, thinking that she was going to be unhappy too, knowing that he didn't love her although perhaps in time he would come to. In the meantime she was going to be the kind of wife he wanted and learn to love little Alicia.

Toogood coughed discreetly at the door. 'If you're ready, sir...'

The dining-room wasn't large but it was elegant, with panelled walls and a circular table and a lovely Georgian sideboard. They ate smoked salmon, fricassee of chicken with asparagus and a soufflé, light as air.

They drank champagne and the professor called Toogood in to drink a glass with them. 'Well, now,' he observed, shedding his dignity for a moment, 'I did think there was something in the wind. I'm sure I wish you both very happy.' He shook their hands and then added, 'I'll serve coffee in the drawing-room, sir.'

It was a beautiful room, due to the lovely pieces with which it was furnished. It crossed her mind that Gijs must have plenty of money but she didn't dwell on the thought. She came from a comfortable home herself and it had been impressed upon her from an early age that money was nice to have but wasn't necessary for happiness. She loved Gijs so much that if he had told her that he was penniless it wouldn't have mattered at all.

They had their coffee by the fire and a fierce-looking cat with a torn ear came and sat between them.

'He doesn't suit this room,' said Beatrice. 'He's a bit battle-scared, isn't he?'

'Willoughby—he's Toogood's pet and constant companion; he keeps me company when I'm here.'

She bent to stroke the cat's head. 'Did he just join the household?'

'In a way, yes. I fished him out of a water butt.'

'Oh, the poor creature, he must be devoted to you.'

'I don't know about that. I think his devotion is given to Toogood, who feeds him.'

The phone by his chair rang and he picked up the receiver and since he spoke Dutch she guessed that it was Alicia. Presently Gijs handed her the phone. 'I have told her that we are to be married but she wants to hear you say so as well.'

Beatrice listened to the childish voice, squeaky with excitement, a jumble of bridesmaid's dresses, her bridal bouquet and when she was going to see Beatrice.

Beatrice about to answer this glanced at Gijs, saw the finger on his lip and said that she wasn't sure but it would be quite soon and presently handed the phone back.

'You don't want her to know?' she asked.

'Occasionally I am called away unexpectedly—I don't want to disappoint her. Shall you phone your mother?'

Beatrice heard her mother's quick breath. 'Darling—what splendid news, and what a lovely surprise.'

'Gijs would like to come with me for the weekend and bring Alicia with him...'

'Of course, we'll love to have them. Is he there? Could I speak to him? Where are you?'

'He's here—at his flat...'

She handed Gijs the phone and he put an arm around her. There was nothing loverlike about it, just a friendly gesture, but it felt nice all the same. She listened to his quiet voice and presently when he rang off she asked, 'You said we might be married as soon as I could be ready. Do you have to go away or have you a great deal of work piling up?'

'Neither. At least no more work than usual and I have several consultations lined up, but all of them in Europe. But do you not agree with me that since we have agreed to marry we might do so without delay? We are both mature people, are we not? I doubt if you will need months of shopping and fussing around with bridesmaids and bridal plans.'

Beatrice felt rage bubbling up inside her. She moved away from his arm and said coldly, 'Even the most mature of brides likes to plan her wedding.'

She was seized and held close. 'Oh, my dear girl, I put that very badly, didn't I?' His voice was full of remorse. 'You are young and beautiful and if you wish to take six months preparing for our wedding then you shall do exactly as you wish and I will wait until you are ready.'

Her rage subsided. Being called young and beautiful had something to do with that; besides, she had no wish for a grand wedding. She said soberly, 'If you wouldn't mind waiting for two or three weeks. We can have a quiet wedding at Little Estling and Alicia can be a bridesmaid. Our friends can come to the church—I expect you have family—will they want to come?'

'Oh, yes. My mother and father, and I have a married sister and some close friends. I think that we need not invite my aunts and uncles, cousins and nieces and nephews— they're legion. We'll meet them all when we go back to Holland.'

A daunting thought, but she would feel better about it once she was married. 'Then we'll go and see Mr Perkins at the weekend?'

'By all means let us do that; once that is settled you can give me a date and I can arrange my work to fit in with it.'

She said diffidently, 'You won't want to stay in England after we're married?'

'Only if you would like that.'

She supposed sadly that a honeymoon hardly fitted into their sensible planning. 'No, not at all. I was thinking about Alicia...'

'She can go back with us; she mustn't miss too much school—she will spend a week or two with my mother and father once the holidays start.'

Beatrice agreed pleasantly, reminding herself that since he wasn't in love with her he would have no desire to have her to himself.

He drove her back to St Justin's presently, saw her to her own door, kissed her cheek and bade her goodnight and went away. If he had had any desire to linger he gave no sign of it.

She wandered round the room, sniffing at the roses. He would be gone again in the morning but he and Alicia would come for her on Saturday. She wondered if she should do something about giving her notice in; he hadn't said any more about that and she had forgotten to ask. She decided to do nothing about it as she got ready for bed which was just as well because the next morning she was sent for by the hospital manager and told that she might leave in a week's time. 'Such exceptional circumstances,' said the manager with a knowing look, 'and the professor being such an important man. Fortunately there is another exchange planned—all that is necessary is for me to bring it forward and while your replacement is here we can select your successor.'

Beatrice expressed suitable gratitude, professed herself quite ready to show whoever was coming what her job entailed and then went back to her work. Gijs, she thought lovingly, certainly knew how to get things done.

They came for her on Saturday morning, the professor unhurried and calm, Alicia bubbling over with excitement. She insisted on exploring the room, pronounced it much too small to live in and wanted to know why Beatrice didn't go and live with her papa.

'Well, I will when we are married,' said Beatrice matter-of-factly. 'I'm still working here, you know.'

It was a watery kind of morning but there was more than a hint of spring in the air now as they drove to Little Estling. Beatrice listened to Alicia chattering to her father and allowed her thoughts to dwell on what she would wear at her wedding.

Her mother and father welcomed them warmly, made much of Alicia, and fell at once to discussing the wedding over their coffee.

'Will you marry here, darling?' asked her mother. 'A summer wedding?'

Beatrice cast a look at the professor, deep in some discussion with her father.

'We rather thought in about three weeks' time—here, of course. A quiet wedding...'

'Well, of course, love, if that's what you want. Your friends will be disappointed and so will the family.'

The two men were listening now and Gijs said smoothly, 'Perhaps we can arrange things to please everyone. It is for Beatrice to decide, of course, but if we had just close family at the church, could there be a reception for your friends afterwards?'

Mrs Crawley brightened. 'That's a good idea. The church is small anyway.'

'If we married fairly early in the morning and had a buffet here?' suggested Beatrice. She frowned. 'But that would be too early for Gijs and Alicia to get here.'

'We'll put up with Derek's people,' he told them. 'Everyone else can stay in Aylesbury.'

Alicia had been listening, sitting on a low stool with Horace stretched out beside her. 'I am to wear a pink frock,' she told the company at large.

'Ah, yes, of course, you will be a bridesmaid, my dear,' observed Mrs Crawley. 'Tell me, what sort of dress is it to be?'

A pleasant topic which kept them occupied until lunch and after that meal Beatrice and Gijs walked down to the village and talked to Mr Perkins, who agreed happily with everything they suggested, advised the professor how to set about getting a special licence and embarked on a short homily concerning the duties of man and wife and got quite carried away and ended with the observation that he had felt romance in the air when he had seen them together at Lady Dowley's party. Beatrice blushed but the professor congratulated him gravely upon his perception, observing that he had had similar feelings.

On their way back Beatrice said tartly, 'You need not have agreed with the rector, you know...'

'What about?' The professor's voice was bland.

'Well, you know, all that about romance.' She turned to frown at him. 'It was very tiresome of you!'

'I stand rebuked,' he told her, still bland. Remind me if at any time in the future I should get a romantic notion into my head. There should be no need of romance between friends.' When she fell silent he added, 'You approve of the arrangements? I'll put a notice in the *Telegraph* and gather my family together—not many; twenty or so, I dare say. How about you?'

'The same, more or less. Mother can invite as many as she likes to the reception—if they all come no one is going to feel left out.'

'A splendid idea. Now, this question of Alicia's frock? Could you get it settled before we go back to Holland. Write it all down and I'll get someone to make it. Nanny will know what to do.'

'That would be a great help—you'll let her choose the colour, won't you?'

'My dear girl, I wouldn't dream of doing otherwise. What about you?'

'Me? Well, I don't really know...'

'Wear white and a bridal veil,' said the professor surprisingly. 'Just this once, indulge me in my romantic fancies.'

'I don't think our wedding will be quite as quiet as we had planned.' She spoke matter-of-factly but her heart had given a happy lurch at his words. For something to say she asked, 'Your sister—she's married? Did she have a big wedding?'

'Indeed she did, six bridesmaids, the choir, ushers, flowers everywhere and two hundred guests. She was living at home with my parents and the place was in an uproar for months beforehand.'

'Well, you won't be here so any uproar need not bother you. We can just meet at the church.'

He stopped a few yards from the house and turned her round and kissed her swiftly. 'Something to which I will look forward,' he told her.

Mrs Crawley, peering cautiously out of the window, smiled happily. They would suit each other very well although she wasn't sure if Beatrice knew that yet. Outwardly they were behaving like any other engaged couple but there was something...

Whatever it was wasn't apparent in Beatrice's manner during the weekend; she was her usual cheerful sensible self and on Sunday as they left the church she had been surrounded by well-wishers all anxious to meet the groom. Even Lady Dowley's two-edged remark that Beatrice was at last going to settle down, and high time too—this with

a sweetly spiteful smile at the professor—
failed to dislodge her smile.

Walking back to her home with her parents
following with Alicia, Gijs said placidly, 'I like
your friends, Beatrice, but must that abom-
inable woman come to our wedding?'

She laughed. 'Lady Dowley? She's a thorn
in everyone's flesh. I don't know why we put
up with her; I dare say it's because she gives
lavish parties.'

'Ah, yes, she made some sickeningly sen-
timental remark about us meeting under her
roof.'

'Well, she'll have to be asked to the reception but there will be lots of people there
so you can avoid her.'

They left that evening after an afternoon
largely taken up with earnest discussions
about Alicia's dress. Her own outfit Beatrice
hadn't mentioned nor did she intend to. Gijs
knew what it would be because he had asked
her to wear white and a veil, and she had given
her mother a broad enough hint to satisfy that
lady's maternal curiousity.

Alone in her flat after an enthusiastic
farewell from Alicia and a coolly friendly one
from Gijs, Beatrice made a pot of tea and sat
down with pen and paper; the wedding was
three weeks away and there was more than

enough to keep her busy until then. Gijs had said that he would come over to England although he wasn't sure when that would be and she still had a week to work at the hospital. She went to bed at length, her more prosaic plans quite swamped with the more interesting prospect of the shopping she needed to do.

Her exchange replacement came two days later and she set her own plans on one side for the moment while she concentrated on her—a nice girl and anxious to please. She heard nothing from Gijs but she hadn't expected to. He wasn't a man to waste time on unnecessary letters; it wasn't as though he were a man in love and anxious to remind her of it. It was her last day at the department when she met Tom crossing the forecourt. He stopped and caught hold of her arm. 'Well, well, you have done well for yourself,' he told her nastily. 'You're no better than I, my dear. Feathered your nest very nicely, haven't you? The man's filthy rich, or didn't you know?'

She took his hand off her arm. 'Goodbye, Tom. I hope everything turns out well for you.' She went on her way and tried to forget what he had said—and didn't succeed.

CHAPTER SEVEN

IT WAS hard for Beatrice to forget Tom's words. There had been no truth in them but they still rankled. She packed the last of her things and got ready for bed, feeling unhappy. When the phone rang she lifted the receiver and said, 'Hello,' her thoughts elsewhere.

'I shall pick you up at nine o'clock tomorrow morning,' said Gijs into her ear, 'and drive you home.'

'Gijs—oh, Gijs, I'm so glad you rang...'

'What's worrying you? Second thoughts—cold feet?'

'Yes, no—I don't know...' She felt like bursting into tears. 'Are you quite sure you want to marry me?'

His voice sounded reassuring. 'Quite sure.' Then he added, 'You've seen Tom.'

'We met accidentally,' she sniffed. 'He made me feel cheap.'

'Don't talk rubbish.' He sounded kind but brisk. 'You have always struck me as being a sensible woman, not given to flights of fancy. Now go to bed like a good girl and be ready for me in the morning.'

'You're here? In London?'

'I'm at home, on the point of leaving for the ferry.'

'You'll be tired...'

'You sound like a wife already. Goodnight, my dear.'

She was up early, ready, with her luggage packed and the room in apple-pie order ready for her successor and had the door open at the first peal of the bell. The professor bent to kiss her cheek, looking like a man who had spent the night in his bed. He was beautifully turned out but then he always was—she wondered momentarily how he managed it and asked if he had had a good journey. 'You've had breakfast? I can make you a cup of coffee...'

He smiled down at her. 'Toogood wouldn't let me out of the flat until I had had breakfast. Are you ready? Do you suppose your mother could give me lunch? I must get back this evening and I don't want to go back to the flat.'

She goggled at him. 'Gijs, you never came over just to drive me home?'

'A pleasure I wouldn't miss for the world,' he told her. 'Let's have some of those bags.'

She had said her goodbyes on the previous evening. She got into the Bentley and only as they drove through the entrance did she realise that she hadn't felt a single pang of regret at leaving St Justin's; rather, her mind was full of the excitement ahead of her. She could hardly believe it, that she would be with Gijs for the rest of their lives. She would have liked to have told him so but he had started a casual conversation which never touched on the serious; she was content to go along with him and the journey went quickly with barely a word about the wedding or their future. He told her that everything had been arranged without enlarging upon that and went on to tell her about Alicia's excitement.

'Has she got her dress?' Beatrice wanted to know.

'Indeed she has. It hangs in her room and is admired ceaselessly. I have been told the details of its making so often that I believe that at a pinch I could sew another one myself.'

She waited for him to ask about her dress, but he didn't.

When they reached her home her father was still busy in his surgery but her mother urged them indoors. 'Leave the luggage for the time being,' she told the professor, 'Take off your coat and come and have some coffee. It's in the kitchen—I've just made some scones...'

Dr Crawley joined them presently and they sat round the table talking until there was neither coffee nor scones left. 'You'll stay the night?' asked Mrs Crawley.

'I'm going back this afternoon, but I'd love to stay to lunch if you'll have me.'

'You poor man, you'll be worn out. You won't have to go to work in the morning, will you?'

'Well, there are one or two things lined up, but I shall be home by late this evening.'

'Do we see you again before the wedding?'

'I shall be too busy, I'm afraid.' He glanced at Beatrice, sitting opposite him. 'I can give you a ring.'

'Yes, of course. Do you want us to do anything about your guests? Where are they to stay and so on? And will they want to be met?'

'I've got rooms for them at the Bell in Aylesbury, I'll be with Derek's people and so will my best man. We shall have to leave the reception about two o'clock—I'm booked on an early evening hovercraft, so we can be home a few hours later. I had thought that we might take Alicia with us but it will make a long day for her—she could travel back with my family on the following day if that doesn't inconvenience you.'

'It sounds a good idea,' agreed Mrs Crawley, reflecting that it would be much more inconvenient for the newly married couple to have a child, however sweet and loved, with them.

Lunch was one of Mrs Crawley's beef casseroles with succulent meat and vegetables topped by dumplings. The professor, being a large man, ate hugely, and Beatrice wondered when he had last had a meal. Breakfast, of course, but before that? He couldn't have had much time to eat during his journey. When they were married, she decided silently, she would make sure that he had his meals regularly.

He left shortly after the meal and Beatrice, throwing an old coat over her shoulders, went out to the car with him.

'Drive carefully,' she begged, 'and do have something to eat. All this travelling must be bad for you.'

He gave her a slow smile. 'When you're at the other end of the travelling, Beatrice, it is good for me. Ah—I almost forgot.' He searched his pockets. 'This...' He put a small case into her hands and she opened it. There was a ring inside, three sapphires surrounded by diamonds, a magnificent piece of jewellery. 'Put this on,' he told her. 'The poesy ring fitted so well that I had this one altered to the same size. It's old-fashioned, for it has been in the family for a long time, but I hope you will wear it.'

He wasn't going to put it on her finger; after a moment she slipped it on above the poesy ring. 'It's beautiful, Gijs, and of course I'll wear it, only may I wear the poesy ring as well?'

'Of course you may, it's yours. You like it so much?'

'Yes.' She spoke soberly and he asked quickly,

'Is something the matter, my dear?'

'No, no, of course not.' She gave him a sweet smile. 'You will ring me when you have time?'

He bent to kiss her. 'Yes, and so will Alicia.'

'Give her my love. You're sure she doesn't mind us marrying?'

'Quite sure, my dear.'

He got into the car and drove away then, lifting a hand as he reached the gate and turned into the road.

Her mother, who had been watching from the drawing-room window, went back to her chair. 'Will they be happy?' she asked her husband urgently.

The doctor lowered his newspaper. 'Why should they not be?' he wanted to know. 'Beatrice is a grown woman with her head screwed on straight, Gijs is a splendid man, respected by the profession, extremely clever and, from what he tells me, more than able to keep Beatrice in great comfort.'

'Yes,' persisted Mrs Crawley, 'but do they love each other?'

Her husband shook out his paper and turned the page. 'That, my dear, is a matter for the two of them, is it not?'

His wife gave a small exasperated noise but as Beatrice came into the room then she turned it into a cough and plunged into the plans for the wedding. 'What about your dress?' she wanted to know. 'Are you going up to London to get it?'

'I thought I would drive over to Bath and get the material and ask Miss Fish to make it for me.'

Miss Fish lived in the village, an elderly body who had worked all her life for a famous couturier in London and now was retired.

'Is it a secret?'

'Not to you, Mother, dear. I thought ivory satin, very plain.' She looked down at her magnificent proportions. 'There's too much of me to have frills and flounces.'

'Long tight sleeves and quite a high neck,' mused her parent.

'Exactly. It's still quite chilly; I don't want to be a mass of goose-pimples.'

'Indeed no. Would you like to borrow my veil?'

'I was going to ask you. Yes, please. It's creamy-coloured and there's that tiny lace edge to it.'

The pair of them became absorbed in the clothes she would need to get and presently her father put down his paper and got out his cheque-book.

'You're bound to see something you don't really need but simply have to have.' He glanced at his wife. 'And you, dear, you will need a new hat, I have no doubt.'

The cheques were generous. Both ladies thanked him suitably and then left him in peace to finish his paper while they sat down to make lists, Mrs Crawley to frown over suitable food for the many friends whom she knew would want to come to the reception and Beatrice to plan clothes which would fit into Gijs's lifestyle. She wasn't sure about that; he had never told her much about his friends or his leisure hours. Perhaps she could ask him when he phoned.

It was two days before he telephoned—two busy days for Beatrice; she had been to Bath, bought the satin for her wedding-dress, been to Miss Fish with it, visited and been visited by almost everyone in the village, all of them eager to see her ring and go into raptures over the professor. Quite the handsomest man they had ever seen and wasn't she a lucky girl?

She agreed with the former and smiled at the latter sentiment. Of course she was lucky; wasn't she going to marry the man she loved? On the other hand, however much he liked her, he wasn't in love with her, was he? Probably another man might have pretended love, but he wasn't a man to pretend. Beatrice, trying various ways of wearing her mother's veil, told herself sensibly that all she needed was patience. After all, he had chosen her for his wife; she must be attractive to him...

He phoned just as she had finished washing her hair so that she went over to the telephone with her head swathed in a towel and icy trickles running down her back.

He wasn't one to waste time on chat. 'I think it might be a good idea if you and your mother and father came over to Aylesbury on the evening before we marry. My people will be at the Bell by then; I'll come over during the afternoon with Alicia—perhaps we might have dinner together so that the families can get to know each other.'

She agreed that it would be a good idea, for there would not be much time to talk at the reception.

'Good, I'm glad you agree. Is there anyone you would like to invite other than your mother and father and George?'

'Well, I have two aunts, elderly and old-fashioned but family-minded, if you know what I mean. Could they come? They'll be at the reception but there will be a lot of people there and they are a bit deaf.'

'Let me have their address and I'll see that they are fetched to the Bell.'

'Thank you, Gijs.' She gave him their address and asked about Alicia.

'In bed. Probably dreaming about her pink dress. And you, Beatrice, are you dreaming too?'

She hadn't expected that. She answered carefully, 'I've just washed my hair,' and when he didn't reply she added reluctantly, 'Well, of course I am a bit. By the time you get here I'll be quite sensible again.'

She thought she heard him sigh. 'I'll be in Brussels for a couple of days—if you need to reach me you can ring here, Bilder will know where I am.'

She put the receiver down and went to tell her mother about the dinner party. 'Gijs will phone again and let me know the time... He said he'd see that the aunts were fetched. I thought it was a good idea if they were there.'

'Quite right, love, it's a splendid idea. Now, what shall I wear? I wonder what his mother is like?'

Beatrice wondered too. Mothers-in-law were reputed to be difficult when it came to their sons' wives. Perhaps she lived near to Gijs, in which case would she be popping in and out every few days to criticise? Beatrice, viewing her future with a pang of doubt, told herself that an interfering mother-in-law wouldn't make any difference; she loved Gijs and nothing else mattered.

The days flew by and became weeks and it was the day before the wedding. The wedding-dress hung in her bedroom, her hair was washed, her hands creamed and manicured. She had gone to bed each night with a special cream guaranteed to eradicate all blemishes from her face. Beatrice was ready. She had given a good deal of thought to what she should wear that evening; it was to be black ties and she had several new dresses from which to choose. She decided on a misty blue dress of crêpe de Chine, what she described to herself as a safe dress since it would be right for almost any occasion after six o'clock. It had long sleeves with a pleated frill at the wrists and a square neckline edged with the same small frill. Suitable for a mother-in-law muttered Beatrice, making sure that everything was just so before going downstairs to join her parents and George.

Lights blazed from the Bell's windows and the foyer was warm and welcoming. Someone took their coats and a moment later the professor came into the hall. Under the blue silk Beatrice's heart lurched into her throat; even if she hadn't fallen in love with him already she told herself, she would have done so now. Dinner-jackets were made for men such as he.

He bent to kiss her cheek and then greeted her parents. 'Everyone is here and so anxious to meet you.' A bellboy opened the door and her mother and father went in to the room beyond and Gijs put a hand on her arm. 'You look beautiful,' he told her quietly. 'Come along.'

Afterwards she had difficulty in remembering that evening. Gijs had led her from one o another of his family. His mother she remembered, though: a massively built lady with a still beautiful and kind face, who had embraced her warmly and beamed her delight. His father too, as tall as his son and still a handsome man. He had kissed her and stood back to look at her. 'I have always said that one daughter wasn't enough and now I have another, exactly the one I would wish for.'

Then there had been a sea of faces, all smiling, and then Alicia had come running to be kissed and then Gijs's sister and after that more faces. Dinner had been a festive affair; she had eaten very little, conscious of Gijs beside her, aware that her own family were enjoying themselves and that the aunts, very dignified in their old-fashioned black silk dresses, were in their element. The party had broken up quite early for the wedding was to be at eleven o'clock in the morning, and she was swept away by Gijs, who was to drive her home, to the accompaniment of voices uttering the predictable remark that the bride needed her beauty sleep.

Gijs hadn't said much as he drove her back, nor had he lingered when they reached the house. He had kissed her swiftly and driven off, over to Derek's home where he was to spend the night. She'd gone indoors feeling let down.

She hadn't expected to sleep, but she did, almost as soon as her head touched the pillow. Her mother, coming quietly with warm milk in case she needed soothing, stood looking at her, lying there with her hair all over the place, dead to the world. Obviously she need not worry about her daughter's pre-wedding nerves. She took the milk back to the kitchen and drank it herself, feeling that her own nerves needed soothing. She would miss Beatrice but she liked Gijs; more than that, she was fond of him, and Beatrice was going to a splendid home and a comfortable future, so why did she feel uneasy? She asked her husband as they got ready for bed.

'You mustn't worry, my dear,' he told her. 'As I have already said, they are both grown-up people who know what they want. They want to marry; I am sure they will never regret it. Now go to sleep, dear. I want you to be the prettiest mother of the bride that the village has ever seen.'

True to tradition, Beatrice had her breakfast in bed, scattering toast crumbs all over the bed and drinking endless cups of tea but without waste of time. The serious business of getting dressed lay ahead of her.

Later, going down the aisle of the church on her father's arm with Alicia, proud in her pink dress, behind her, Beatrice decided that the entire village, invited or not, had crammed into its pews. They were only a blur, though, for her eyes were on Gijs's broad shoulders and when he turned to look at her she smiled happily at him.

He smiled back while he studied the pretty face under the veil and the simple satin dress. She was indeed very beautiful.

The ceremony was a simple one but the congregation sang the hymns with gusto and those who hadn't been able to get into the church were waiting outside its door, watching while photos were taken and then hurling confetti as they went down the path to the cars.

In the car Beatrice said, 'I'm afraid it wasn't very quiet after all.'

'But delightful—I feel very married.' He turned to smile at her and picked up her hand and kissed its palm. 'Alicia managed very well, didn't she?'

'Splendidly, and she looked so pretty...' There was no time to say more for they had reached her home, joined almost immediately by the family and very soon engulfed by guests.

Gijs stayed with her but there was little chance to talk, well-wishers jostled around them and Alicia was never far away. It was like a dream, thought Beatrice, cutting the cake with Gijs, smiling and talking and not sure if it were all true, aware only that she was married to Gijs and that she loved him so nothing else would matter any more.

She went away to change presently with Alicia sitting on the bed, gabbling away in two languages, regretful that she wouldn't be going with them but excited at the idea of staying with her grandparents at Aylesbury.

Presently the pair of them went downstairs again to find Gijs waiting for them. He had changed from his morning dress to a tweed suit and was surrounded by a laughing group of people but as they reached the hall he came to meet them and she could see the approval in his eyes. She was wearing a brown and oatmeal Tattersall check suit with a blouse of oyster silk shantung. She had tied a beautiful Gucci scarf around her neck and she wore brown suede shoes with low heels and on her neat head she was wearing a little brown cap made by the magic-fingered Miss Fish. She knew that she looked nice but she was glad to see his approval.

She knew that he never lingered over goodbyes; they were said with well mannered brevity and she took her cue from him and made her own parents goodbye without more ado, said the right things to her new in-laws and got into the Bentley. There was a little delay then while Alicia poked her head through the windows for a last kiss and then they were driving away, going slowly through the crowds surrounding the car.

They were clear of the village before Gijs spoke. 'A day to remember,' he observed. 'How kind everyone was, even Lady Dowley, though I must say she asks a great many questions.'

'Did she cross-examine you too? She wanted to know so much...'

'I know. Given a little encouragement she would have asked the state of my bank account.'

'She reminded me what a lucky young woman I was...'

He glanced at her smiling. 'I believe it is the groom who is the lucky one. Am I not right?'

She said soberly, 'I hope we shall both be lucky.'

'No doubt of it. A pity we can't do the whole thing again so that I could take a good

look at you at my leisure. All I had were brief
glimpses.'

Beatrice laughed. 'You can study the photos
when they arrive.'

He had allowed good time for their journey;
they stopped for a leisurely tea, he had driven
down to Beaconsfield and so to the M25 but
turned off at Sevenoaks, making his way
across country through country roads until
he stopped at Tenterden at the White Hart
Hotel. They discussed their wedding at some
length over tea, rather as if, thought Beatrice
wistfully, they were old friends talking about
someone else's wedding and not a newly
married couple, holding hands and whis-
pering lovingly. Not that Gijs would do that,
however much in love he was.

The Channel was absolutely calm when they
crossed and there were still two hours or more
of daylight left. In the car once again Gijs
drove fast, out of France, out of Belgium and
across the border into Holland.

'Tired?' he wanted to know. 'We shan't be
long now. You will be glad of a quiet day
tomorrow.'

'You'll be there too?'

'I've a couple of days free; in any case I
shall be working in Leiden for a week or more
so I shall be at home each evening. You will

have the day to find your way around and if you like we can go out in the evening.'

'When will Alicia come home?'

'On Sunday; I—we will fetch her and we can have the day together.'

'One day, when you have time,' said Beatrice firmly, 'I should like to know exactly what kind of work you do. I used to hear this and that at St Justin's and it sounded so interesting.'

'It is. I shall enjoy explaining it to you. How pleasant to come home to someone who will listen to me grumbling about the day's work.'

It was strange and a little frightening to get out of the car at his house and remember that it would be her home too but she was given little time to reflect upon that; Bilder was there at the door, holding it wide open so that the light from the hall streamed out to meet them.

There was a small crowd in the square, as near the gates to the house as they could come, and Gijs said softly, 'A welcoming group from the village,' and turned her round to face them. He said something to those nearest him and there was laughter and clapping and a small child was pushed forward to thrust a bunch of flowers at Beatrice. It was so unexpected that she wasn't sure what to do; she bent and kissed the rather grubby cheek and smiled at them all and said quite inadequately, 'Thank you very much.'

It seemed that she had done the right thing, for there was a general chorus of cheerful voices before Gijs spoke again and took her arm and walked to the door. The next thing that happened was even more unexpected; he lifted her without effort and carried her over the threshold, set her down neatly and waved to his audience and allowed Bilder to close the door.

'Well!' said Beatrice, very much surprised, and then smiled again because Bilder and his wife and two sturdy girls were standing there shaking hands with Gijs and presently with her.

'You brushed through that very nicely,' murmured the professor, taking her coat and urging her towards the drawing-room where they were met by Fred, falling about with delight at the sight of them.

'I think we need a drink,' said Gijs. 'I must be out of practice...'

'Oh—was I very heavy?'

'Out of practice at getting married,' he said.

He spoke lightly and she reminded herself that though she was his wife she was his friend, a dear friend perhaps, but still only that.

They drank champagne and sat for a while, talking about their day until Gijs said, 'Nanny will be waiting for us; shall we go and see her now before we have supper? I'll take you to your room as we go.'

They went up the curving staircase together and on the broad landing at the front of the house he opened double doors, mahogany with elaborate carvings above them. The room was very large and had long windows opening on to a balcony of wrought iron. It over-looked the square but sufficiently far away to keep its privacy and to make sure of that there were heavy lace curtains at the windows and old rose brocade draped on either side. The bed coverlet was of the same colour and the dressing-table and tallboys were of satinwood with exquisite marquetry.

Beatrice revolved slowly, looking at it all. 'It is beautiful...'

'I'm glad you like it; everything here is very old, I believe nothing has been changed for a very long time. The bathroom is through that door, my room is beyond and there's a dressing-room on the other side.'

He waited patiently while she looked at everything and presently they went up an-other flight of stairs to where Nanny had her own bed-sitting-room.

She got up as they went in and kissed them both and wished them happy. 'I didn't come down when you got back,' she explained. 'I guessed there would be a few people from the village wanting to have a look at your bride. Was the wedding as quiet as you had hoped for?' She sat down between them. 'And was Alicia good?'

'She was quite perfect,' said Beatrice, 'and she looked lovely. What a very pretty dress—she looked sweet.'

They talked for a bit and then Beatrice said, 'Shall I come and see you tomorrow and tell you all the details? We've had some photos taken too...'

'That'll be fine. You'll be wanting your suppers, the pair of you—getting married is a tiring business, so I've been told.' She got up and went to a chest of drawers. 'Before you go, I've a wee present for you both. I wasn't going to send it.'

She gave Beatrice a packet wrapped in tissue paper and watched as she unwrapped it. There was an exquisitely embroidered tray cloth inside. 'For your early morning tea tray,' explained Nanny. 'The pair of you can share it of a morning.'

Beatrice found her voice. 'It's beautiful, Nanny—may I call you Nanny? How exquisitely you've embroidered it—we shall take such care of it—the morning tea will taste all the better for it.' She kissed the elderly cheek. 'Thank you very much. It's the nicest present we've had, isn't it, Gijs?'

He agreed gravely and added his thanks and presently they went back downstairs and into the dining-room where Bilder was waiting for them beside a table decked with crisp damask, crystal and silver. There was a bowl of red roses in the centre and candles in silver candelabra on either side. Beatrice said, 'Oh, how lovely,' and smiled at Bilder and didn't look at Gijs. It seemed that everyone was determined to make the occasion as romantic as possible, excepting, of course, Gijs.

Thinking about it afterwards, she couldn't remember what she ate—it had been delicious and they had had more champagne before going back to the drawing-room with Fred hugging their heels, to sit by the wide hearth until Gijs suggested that she might like to go to bed. 'You must be tired,' he told her kindly. 'Is there anything you would like? At what time would you like your morning tea? I usually breakfast at eight o'clock, sometimes earlier—would you like to have yours in bed?'

'Only when I'm ill. Does Alicia have breakfast with you?'

'No, with Nanny, but she comes to say good morning before I leave or she goes to school.'

'I'd like to have breakfast with you,' said Beatrice, 'I won't talk, and you can read your letters in peace. You must tell me how you like to live and I'll fit in.' She made her voice sound matter-of-fact; he had said that their marriage would be one of friendship and mutual liking and she realised that that was exactly what he intended it to be. She would have to work hard at making him love her but she was sure that she would succeed. Patience and a little female guile. She gave him a beaming smile, offered a cheek for his kiss and went up to her lovely room. Where, presently, she cried herself to sleep.

There was no getting away from the fact that they enjoyed each other's company; they spent the next day going over the house at their leisure, spending time with Nanny, taking Fred for a long walk and on their return stopping to talk to the various people they met on their way. Of course, she was quite unable to understand much of what was said, but smiling seemed sufficient and from time to time Gijs translated rapidly.

The next day was just as delightful. There was so much she wanted to know and he took the time and trouble to tell her. Life for her, she could see, was going to be pleasant. Gijs already had many friends and a large family and there would be a social life although he stressed that his work would always come first. 'I do like my friends to dine here occasionally and there are various functions which I can't avoid—I'm sure you'll enjoy them.'

'There is Alicia too,' she told him. 'I hope we shall be real friends. I'll take great care not to upset Nanny...'

'Nanny approves of you; besides, she isn't so young and it will be a great help to her if you take Alicia walking and so on—Nanny gets tired.'

'You wouldn't send her away?'

'Certainly not. When Alicia has outgrown her, she shall stay on; there is always something for her to do in a house this size—she loves needlework and mending and she has any number of friends in Leiden.'

'That's all right then. Has Alicia many friends?'

'Hundreds and thousands, or so it seems when she has them to tea. I try not to be at home then.'

They were in his study, she in a big chair by the fire while he sat at his desk, going through his post. She would miss him tomorrow when he went off to work, she thought, but then it would be Sunday and they would fetch Alicia. She put a hand out to scratch Fred's head and the phone rang.

She moved to go but Gijs held up a hand as he took off the receiver. It must be an old friend, she guessed, for he sounded amused and pleased. He talked for some time and when he put the receiver down at last he said, 'That was a very old friend—Mies van Trott— she wants to come and see us. I think you'll like her, I've asked if she will dine with us one day next week so that you can get to know each other.'

He was sitting back in his chair, watching her, and she knew that; she made herself look interested and pleased and said, 'Oh, how nice. I'm sure I shall like her.'

She uttered the fib with a smile and Gijs frowned slightly.

'You're happy, Beatrice?' he asked. 'These two days have proved that we can enjoy life together, have they not? That we are well suited to each other? At the moment there is no need for more.'

'I'm very happy, Gijs.' She spoke steadily, looking at him with a quiet face. 'I'm content to live as we are—there's no hurry.'

Getting someone to fall in love with you, she reflected, wasn't something which could be done overnight; it would take weeks, months, perhaps years.

She got to her feet. 'The *dominee* is coming to tea, isn't he? I'll go and tidy myself.'

He watched her go, his face without expression.

After Gijs had gone the next morning she felt a little panic-stricken; supposing someone called and they didn't speak English? Supposing she missed her way when she took Fred for his walk? Supposing Gijs had an accident in the car? Supposing..! She stopped herself firmly and went to say good morning to Nanny and to listen to her talking about Alicia. After that there was the kitchen to visit and some flowers to arrange and letters to write. She was her sensible self by lunchtime and took Fred for a long walk afterwards. She was a little afraid that he might chase chickens or cats but he pranced along beside her, the picture of meekness. She gave him a biscuit from her tea tray because he had been so good.

At six o'clock Gijs came home and the day, which had seemed rather long, became perfect.

CHAPTER EIGHT

THEY fetched Alicia the next day. Gijs's parents lived at den Haag, in a solid mansion on the outskirts of the town. It was old but not as old as his house at Aaledijk.

It was the custom in the family, he explained to Beatrice, for the eldest son to live there when he married until he in his turn moved out for his own son. There was a house in the country too, in the wooded country north of Arnhem; the whole family used it from time to time. He added carelessly that he owned a small cottage in Brittany; they might all go there in the summer.

Beatrice said 'how nice' in a faint voice. There was a great deal she didn't know about Gijs.

Nothing could exceed the warmth of their welcome. Half strangled by Alicia's delighted hug, Beatrice was in turn embraced by her in-laws and a number of other persons whose names she couldn't hope to remember, cousins from Zutphen and aunts and uncles from

Meppel. She was only vaguely aware of these two places; once she had settled in she would have to get hold of a map of Holland and reread the books Gijs had given her. If she felt like a fish out of water she did her best not to let it show and certainly not for one moment was she made to feel that she wasn't a close member of the family. They had lunch in the old-fashioned dining-room with its enormous sideboard and massive oblong table, and Fred, flanked by her father-in-law's Labrador and her mother-in-law's Scottie, sat like a furry statue, watching every mouthful they ate.

They left soon after lunch since they were to have tea with Nanny and since Alicia didn't stop talking for the whole of the return journey Beatrice was able to pursue her own thoughts for a good deal of the time. They weren't unhappy; she was married to the man she loved and she felt real affection for Alicia, and, once she got used to it, she was going to be perfectly content at Aaledijk. It was the knotty question of how to make Gijs fall in love with her which occupied her. Learning to speak and understand Dutch was a must; to get to know his friends and family and entertain them as he would wish was important too. She reviewed her wardrobe and decided that when she had the opportunity she would add to it; she had money of her own but he had given her credit cards and a thick roll of banknotes and told her briskly that in future he would provide for her. 'As soon as I have the time,' he had told her, 'I will arrange for you to have an account at my bank and if you need more money you only have to ask.'

She had thanked him meekly, sensing that a refusal would touch his pride.

Back home they went straight up to Nanny and, once the first excitement was over, bore her downstairs to have tea. Bilder had set it out on a circular table in a charming little room at the back of the house; a proper tea, declared Nanny happily, sitting down to bread and butter, scones and jam and a magnificent cake which she herself had baked in honour of their return. The tea was hot and strong, just as Nanny liked it, and they sat for a long time, going over the wedding once again for Alicia's benefit, but presently the child was borne off upstairs. 'School tomorrow,' Gijs reminded her. 'I'll take you as I go.'

He went to his study then and Beatrice went off to the drawing-room and sat by the fire; she had a magazine on her lap but she didn't read it. Tomorrow, she decided, she would write letters, take Fred for a walk and perhaps buy something at the village shop. The sooner she made a proper start with her new language, the better... She didn't hear the professor come into the room and he stood for a moment, looking at her profile. He crossed the room and bent to kiss her cheek. 'Had you planned something for tomorrow? Alicia will be at school till half-past three. Would you like to come with me to Leiden? I'll be at the hospital all the morning but I'm sure there's some shopping you might like to do—we could have lunch together. I'll drive you back here. Bilder can take the other car and fetch Alicia and I'll be home just after six o'clock.'

Her rather desperate plans flew out of her head. 'Oh, Gijs, I'd like that very much and there are a few things I need—a dictionary—one with sentences, you know "I'm lost" or "where is the bus station"? Something like that...'

He sat down beside her, laughing. 'Better still, I'll find someone to give you lessons. You have a smattering already, have you not? But you need conversation.'

'Also how to write letters and go shopping.'

'All in good time. We shall probably get invited out a good deal—everyone will want to meet you.' He stretched out in his chair and Fred leaned against his legs. 'Will you come to the hospital at half-past twelve to-morrow? I'll take the car—it will be quicker. I want you to choose a car—you must have one of your own—I'm away from home quite a lot and you must be free to go where you want.'

She stammered a little. 'You're very kind and generous, Gijs. Thank you very much. What sort of car?'

'Whichever you prefer, my dear.'

She was up early the next morning, but not as early as Gijs. She saw him striding across the watermeadows at the side of the house with Fred racing ahead of him and wished that she was with them. It was a fine day. She got into a pleated plaid skirt and a white silk blouse, sensible shoes and, with a corduroy jacket over her arm, went down to breakfast. Alicia met her at the top of the staircase and they went down together, hand in hand, en-joying their usual bilingual conversation and laughing a great deal.

The professor was standing by the table leafing through his post and Alicia ran to him and lifted her small face for his kiss. 'Now kiss Beatrice,' she demanded, so he did, a cool brief kiss on a cheek, so that Beatrice was forced to the conclusion that he was merely obliging his daughter. She wished him good morning, settled Alicia in her chair to start her breakfast and poured the coffee.

Gijs handed her several letters as he took his cup. 'Invitations,' he told her, 'and letters from England. We will go through the invitations together later on but you must be longing to read the others. There is this too——' He handed her a large, strangely wrapped package.

The wedding photos. She opened it and they studied them in turn.

'Very nice. We'll decide how many we want later too, shall we? How about letting Nanny see them and she can pass them on to Bilder and the staff?'

Beatrice stuffed her own letters into her handbag; she could read them later. 'I'll take them now. They're very good ...'

'Don't be long. We're leaving in five minutes.'

Alicia went to a small school in the centre of Leiden and Beatrice got out of the car at the same time. Gijs got out too, walked with them to the school door and watched his small daughter skip inside. He touched Beatrice on her arm lightly. 'You'll be all right? If you want to, come to the hospital when you're ready. The porter will take you somewhere quiet until I'm ready.'

'Otherwise half-past twelve,' said Beatrice.

'Yes.' He smiled down at her and for a moment she thought that he was going to kiss her, but of course he never would do that in the middle of Leiden. 'Go to the end of this street and turn left, that's the Oude Singel—will you know where you are then?'

'Yes, thank you. Don't make yourself late, Gijs.'

His mouth twitched. She saw that and went pink. 'Sorry, of course you don't have to watch the clock.' She smiled a goodbye and walked away. The professor watched her until she had reached the road end and turned the corner before getting into his car and driving away.

Beatrice spent a pleasant morning; there were some excellent bookshops and she spent a long time choosing a phrase book, leafing through the magazines and buying a businesslike notebook which she thought rather vaguely might help with her study of the Dutch language. This done, she had coffee and took herself off to more shops—postcards for various friends who would expect them, some wool and knitting needles, a miniature doll, dressed in the height of fashion, which she thought Alicia might like, and a silk scarf which she was unable to resist.

In good time she made her way to the hospital. It seemed strange to go through its doors as a visitor and a little embarrassing to be addressed importantly as Mevrouw van der Eekerk by the head porter and led away to sit in a side room. The professor, she was told, would be with her within a few minutes.

Which he was, coming quietly into the room, calm and immaculate, just as though he hadn't spent a busy morning and was faced with an even busier afternoon. They went out to the car together and he drove to a more modern area of the town, parked outside a large garage and showroom and got out to open her door.

They were expected; the salesman took them at once to several smaller cars and stood by, saying very little while the professor looked them over.

'Any one of these, Beatrice, or if you don't care for them we'll see what else can be got for you.'

Her eye had fallen at once on a maroon-coloured car. 'That one,' she said without hesitation. 'It's made by Rover, isn't it? I should like to have it very much.'

Her husband looked amused. 'You're very certain. Have you driven one before?'

'No—I like the colour!'

'As good a reason as any,' observed the professor with a straight face and turned away to engage the salesman in talk. Presently he came over to where she was examining the car. 'They'll deliver it this afternoon; you are to try it out. If you don't like it we will exchange it for any other model.'

'Oh, I'm sure I shall like driving it. It's beautiful. Thank you very much, Gijs.'

They left the showroom and went back to the heart of the town to the Bistro de la Cloche, where they ate omelettes stuffed with mushrooms and drank delicious coffee, wasting no time over them since Gijs was going to drive her back to Aaledijk before he started his afternoon's work.

'Outpatients?' asked Beatrice, wanting to show an interest.

'Not until four o'clock. Before that I have several patients to see for the first time—referred to me by their own doctors.'

As he drove her back home she asked, 'Is Mies van Trott coming tomorrow? You said you would ask her to have dinner with us.'

'I'll bring her back with me when I come—
he lives at Valkenburgh. I can pick her up
on my way back.'

She hoped that he would tell her more
about this old friend of his, but he asked her
how she had spent her morning instead.

Back at Aaledijk he got out of the car to
open her door as he always did, made some
remark about enjoying her afternoon, got
back into the car and drove away again with
a casual wave of the hand. She had no reason
to be put out; all the same Beatrice felt her
good spirits slipping. They had started to slip
when he had mentioned Mies van Trott and
somehow the briskness of his goodbye had
made it worse. He had, she reflected, never
wasted time on his goodbyes but he had the
air of a man who felt relief at getting rid of
her.

She mustn't fancy things, she told herself
firmly, nor must she be sorry for herself. She
had married him because she loved him and
she must learn to conform to his ideas of a
wife. Friends, he had said, good companions,
enjoying the same pleasures. She went indoors, collected a delighted Fred and took him
for a walk, and presently when she had had
tea she sat down at the walnut bureau in the
small sitting-room and wrote cards to her

friends. Tomorrow she would go to the village and post them and try out her fragmental Dutch in the village shop and post office.

Then Gijs and Alicia came home and there was laughter and cheerful chatter about the day and they played Snakes and Ladders before the little girl went to bed. It seemed very quiet when she had left them and Beatrice was glad of the wool and knitting needles she had bought in Leiden. She began to cast on stitches as though her life depended upon it.

The professor sat in his chair, reading the *Haagsche Post* and at the same time watching Beatrice. She looked beautiful, sitting so serenely opposite him, absorbed in her work. He said, 'Do you suppose we might have a salmon mousse tomorrow evening? Mies loves it.'

'Of course, I'll go and see Mevrouw Bilder presently. What else would you suggest?' She looked up and smiled at him. 'Is there anything else Mies likes specially?'

'Beef—and she has a passion for French fries. She's small and slim and eats whatever she likes without gaining an ounce.'

Beatrice became conscious of her own splendid shape. She swallowed a peevish reply and remarked placidly that Mies was a lucky girl.

'Hardly a girl...'

'She sounds nice,' said Beatrice untruthfully. 'Has she never married?'

'No.'

Something in his voice caused her to go on briskly, 'I'm going to the post office tomorrow to try out my Dutch.'

'Ah, I almost forgot. There is a Juffrouw Blanke ready to start your lessons whenever you want. She will phone you in the morning. She's a retired schoolteacher and lives in Leiden. It would be easier for her if you drove into Leiden. She suggested three times a week fairly early in the morning.'

'Thank you, I am looking forward to learning Dutch. Shall I pick up Alicia each day? She comes out of school at half-past three, doesn't she?'

'She'd like that, and it would get you used to our roads. Bilder will always go if you want to do something else. I'm sure you will make friends soon enough and want to spend some time with them.'

She had finished her casting on. She put down the needles and bent to tickle Fred's furry head. He closed his little yellow eyes and hung his tongue out as far as it would go and sighed hugely.

'You have a loving slave for life,' observed the professor and picked up his newspaper again.

A pity he didn't entertain the same feelings for her as his dog did, thought Beatrice.

She went in search of Bilder presently, who in turn fetched his wife so that the business of making the salmon mousse could be discussed. The menu settled to everyone's satisfaction, Bilder observed, 'Juffrouw van Trott is a lady of charm, *mevrouw*, much liked by everyone.'

Except me, thought Beatrice, and went back to sit with Gijs and discuss the day's news with intelligence. It was a task she had set herself each morning, to read the *Daily Telegraph*, which Gijs had delivered for her, and to wrestle with the headlines of the Dutch newspapers, so that if he should choose to comment on the state of the world she at least had a good idea of what he was talking about. There were shelves of books in his study; she had every intention of reading up as much information about haematology as she could digest, so that she would be able to ask about his work when he came home each evening.

Juffrouw Blanke phoned the next morning. Her voice sounded exactly what Beatrice had expected it to be—a schoolteacher's—but her

English was faultless and she was willing to give Beatrice lessons whenever it was convenient. They arranged for three lessons a week at half-past nine, and she was warned in a manner reminiscent of her old headmistress's voice that she must be prepared to do a considerable amount of study at home.

Well, it was a step in the right direction, reflected Beatrice, putting the phone down. To speak and understand the same language as her husband and her friends would help her not to feel at such a disadvantage.

With Gijs and Alicia already gone, she took herself, with Fred in close attendance, down to the village, where she practised her Dutch on a rather bewildered shopkeeper and returned to eat her solitary lunch. She got into her car later that afternoon and drove to Leiden to fetch Alicia from school. She achieved this without mishap, with Fred on the back seat to give her support, and by then it was time to change into something suitable for the evening. She had left it rather late since she and Nanny and Alicia had had a game of Ludo after Alicia's tea, but she scrambled into a jersey dress and elegant shoes, did her hair carefully and made up her face even more carefully. She was sitting in the drawing room, knitting, the very picture of domesticity, when Gijs came home with their guest.

Beatrice had a very clear picture in her head as to what Mies van Trott would look like—small and dark and pretty, with a girlish voice and expensive up-to-date clothes. She was so wrong that just for an instant, as Gijs and Mies came into the room, she could only stand wordlessly, trying to look the part of the delighted hostess.

Mies van Trott was small, true enough, but she was blonde with piled-up hair, gathered on top of her head in a carefully careless style which Beatrice had never been able to achieve. She wasn't pretty, her nose was thin and sharp, her mouth was wide and her eyes, brilliantly blue, were small. Probably her dress was an expensive one but it was too tight and she had thick ankles.

All this Beatrice took in in one lightning glance as she crossed the room.

'There you are, my dear,' observed the professor smoothly. 'Let me introduce Mies to you. Mies, this is Beatrice, my wife.'

The two of them shook hands and Beatrice said quickly, 'How nice to meet you, Mies. I've heard so much about you. Alicia knows you are to be here and I promised that she could come and say good night before she goes to bed.'

'We're old friends,' said Mies, and smiled. 'I'd love to see her.'

'Come and sit down and I'll fetch her presently. Hasn't it been a pleasant day? I went down to the village and the sun was lovely.'

She looked up and found Gijs's eyes upon her; he wasn't smiling but she knew that he was laughing behind his bland expression. When in doubt, talk about the weather.

Mies was willing to go along with her. They discussed the climate at some length until Beatrice said, 'I'll fetch Alicia, shall I?' and went upstairs, glad of a moment's respite. The trouble was, she thought that she was going to like Mies.

Alicia went bounding down the staircase to fling herself at her father and then at Mies. 'It's ages since I saw you,' she began in English, and then switched to her own tongue so that Beatrice had no idea what she was saying. It was her father who suggested quietly that she should speak English so that Beatrice could understand their conversation.

'I really don't mind——' began Beatrice and was interrupted by Alicia throwing her arms around her neck and telling her that she was sorry. 'You mustn't worry,' said the moppet.

'You'll soon learn Dutch now that you're married to Papa.'

'That remains to be seen,' said Beatrice, 'and now how about going to bed?'

She took the child upstairs again and when she came down Gijs was pouring drinks and the talk was of the trivial happenings in the village, local politics and light-hearted comments from Mies about Fred. Never once, during the whole evening, did either she or Gijs mention their friendship or any mutual friends.

At the table when Bilder served the salmon mousse, Mies cried, 'Oh, how lovely—my favourite. However did you know, Beatrice?'

'Gijs told me . . .'

'Oh, Gijs, fancy you remembering.' She turned to Beatrice 'and your Mevrouw Bilder makes the best mousse in the world.' She asked Gijs, 'How long has she been with you, Gijs? It must be years and years.'

'The Bilders came before I married Zalia; I can't remember exactly when. We would be lost without them, wouldn't we, Beatrice?'

'You'll be entertaining again, I suppose,' said Mies. 'Gijs has so many friends. Let me know if I can help in any way, Beatrice.'

Beatrice thanked her sweetly. It would be the last thing she would do.

Later, watching the tail-lights of the Bentley dwindling down to the village, Beatrice wondered if the evening had been a success. Was Mies even now discussing her with Gijs? She shunned the thought at once; Gijs wouldn't do that. He had married her for a number of reasons but he wouldn't discuss them with anyone. Not even a very old friend. Not really so old, reflected Beatrice, going back to sit by the fire and worry away at some knitting. Mies wasn't all that old, in her thirties—but she had no looks to speak of. However, men, she cautioned herself, did not always fall in love with a pretty face.

She was knitting again by the time Gijs got back. 'Still up?' he asked cheerfully as he came into the room. 'Would you like anything before you go to bed? Coffee or a drink?'

She stuck the knitting needles into the wool. 'No, thank you. I was just going up.'

'You enjoyed the evening?'

'Very much. Mies is a nice person...'

He looked as though he was about to say something. It was as she got up and went to the door that he remarked that he had some reading to do before he too could go to bed. 'Sleep well,' he said and kissed her cheek.

She wished him goodnight in a quiet voice. Halfway up the staircase she paused and lent over the bannisters. Gijs was standing at the foot of the staircase. She said in a rush, 'Gijs, could Bilder fetch Alicia tomorrow afternoon? I thought I'd like to take the car and explore a bit—after lunch, just for an hour or two. I'm not sure where so it might be better if he fetched her in case I forget the time.'

'By all means, Beatrice. There's a map in the pocket by the driver's seat. The tank's full; more than enough for an afternoon's run.'

She waited for him to tell her to take care, or come home safely, or any other comforting remark she might have expected from him, but he had no more to say and she went on up the staircase, unaware that he still stood there, watching her with a frowning face.

Presently he went to his study and sat at his desk with Fred lying beside his chair. He made no attempt to read the pile of papers before him but sat deep in thought until the Georgian bracket clock mounted on the wall chimed a muted musical midnight. He got up then, let Fred out for a last run, saw him to his basket in the kitchen and went quietly to his room.

Beatrice, still lying awake, heard him.

The idea of going for a drive had been on the spur of the moment; on second thoughts, she didn't particularly want to go, but she had told Gijs that she was going, so she would. She walked Fred in the morning, had coffee with Nanny, gossiping comfortably about new dresses for Alicia, then she had lunch and went to get her coat. It was a wintry day; there had been a frost overnight but there was no sign of rain or snow; Bilder, coming to tell her that he had brought the car round to the front door for her, cast a thoughtful eye at the sky and warned her not to go too far. 'It is not good, this sky, *mevrouw*. It is really better if you do not go.'

She reassured him. 'I've driven for years, Bilder, and I'll stay on the main roads.' She got in and drove away. The car ran like a dream. She settled back in the seat. She knew where she was going; there was pretty country, according to her guide book, south of Amersfoort, and that town was only fourteen miles from Utrecht, a city not much more than half an hour on the motorway.

She bypassed Utrecht and took the road to Amersfoort. The guide book had been right, even on a wintry day the country was charming. There was no need to go into the town; she turned south on to heathland. The

road was good and there was hardly any
traffic. Ahead of her she could see wooded
country but when she reached a crossroads
she stopped and looked at her map. A country
road, she supposed, running in a semicircle
round the heath. It looked interesting and it
was still early afternoon. She turned the car
into it driving slowly.

She had travelled four or five miles when
it began to rain, and, unlike normal rain, it
froze as it reached the ground. She went into
a skid, righted the car and drove on very
slowly; it seemed the lesser of two evils, for
to have stopped on the icy surface would have
been hazardous.

The rain, like steel rods, made it difficult
to see ahead of her. She rounded a corner with
caution and very slowly slithered to a halt.
There a hundred yards ahead of her two cars
were tangled together, blocking the road.
Beatrice opened her door and put a tentative
foot outside. The surface of the road was like
an ice rink. She got out cautiously, hung on
to the side of the car for as long as possible
and then began a hazardous journey to the
cars. It was impossible to hurry although she
could hear someone shouting. Even at a
snail's pace she fell down several times; by

the time she reached the cars she ached all over.

The cars had their bonnets interlocked and as she reached the nearest car a furious elderly female face thrust itself out of the open window. At least the face's owner wasn't dead or even badly injured, thought Beatrice, since its owner was in full spate. She waited for a pause in the stream of words coming from the car and said, 'Sorry, I don't speak Dutch,' and edged her way carefully along the car to look in the driver's seat. The man was unconscious but breathing; she opened the door and switched off the engine and, although she wanted to take a look at him, made her way to the second car. There was a young man slumped over the wheel but no one else. She hauled him back from the wheel, turned off that engine too and took a look at him. He mumbled something, which was a relief, and she stood, clinging to the car, wondering what she should do. It was a lonely road and it would soon be dusk. She switched on all the lights, edged back to the other car and switched on those too, taking no notice of the querulous voice from the back seat.

The rain was easing and surely there would be dozens of accidents in the area; the police would be on the alert. As far as she could see there wasn't a farm in sight. She went back to the young man and was relieved when he roused himself at her touch. 'OK?' asked Beatrice for lack of a better word. He nodded, and smiled a little. She went back to the other man again; there was no sign of injury, but he was still unconscious. The elderly passenger was still talking. Beatrice put her head through the window and said, 'Oh, do be quiet,' which did no good at all but eased her feelings. She mustn't panic, she told herself firmly. The rain had stopped at last and the road must be used even if infrequently. She climbed into the car beside the unconscious man and took his pulse. It was reassuringly strong. It was dark now and it seemed darker because of the car's lights. At least they would show up, she thought hopefully.

It was a police helicopter which spotted them. It landed in a nearby field and a large calm police officer opened the door as the woman in the back started to pour out a flood of words at him.

Beatrice got out. 'Do you speak English' Yes, good...' She explained what had happened, and he took out his portable phone and spoke into it.

'There will be an ambulance. You know these people?'

'No. My car's up the road. I stopped to help.'

'Your name, please?'

She told him. 'My husband will be worried... May I go and will you tell me the quickest way to get back?'

'Your phone number, *mevrouw*? I will telephone.'

Which he did, and then passed the phone to her. Gijs's voice, cold and angry and quiet. 'Beatrice, have you any idea...? Stay where you are in your car. I'll be there as soon as possible.'

He didn't wait for her to answer. She thanked the officer and walked carefully back to the car and got in and sat behind the wheel. Gijs was angry; she had never heard his voice like that, and he hadn't said that he was glad that she had been found. She sat there weeping quietly, getting very cold.

The ambulance came and more police, this time in cars. She closed her eyes because her head ached and then opened them as Gijs opened her door.

She stared at him; he must be very angry, his face was white and his mouth was a hard thin line. She tried to think of something soothing to say and couldn't.

The professor stood looking down at her.
She was quite lacking in looks, her pale face
smeared in tears, her hair all over the place,
the tip of her delightful nose pink, her grey
eyes red-rimmed. He wanted to shake her until
her teeth rattled but more than that he wanted
to hold her close and kiss her and tell her what
a beautiful girl she was. He said in a gentle
voice, 'You must be very cold. Come along,
the car's warm and we'll soon be home.'

'I can't leave this car...'

He reached over and took the key from the
dashboard. 'Bilder can fetch it in the
morning.' He scooped her out with a large
arm and shoved her carefully into the Bentley
and Fred's whiskery face greeted her. For
some reason that made her want to cry again.
Gijs put a large handkerchief into her hand.
'I'll just have a word with the police,' he told
her and by the time he came back she had
wiped her face and pushed her hair away from
her face. He got in beside her and made her
drink some brandy from a flask. 'We won't
talk now,' he said in the same gentle voice.
'It's a bit tricky driving.'

She was content to sit silent with his reassuring bulk beside her and Fred's gentle rum-
blings from the back seat.

The roads were still icy but Gijs drove with calm assurance. The car's warmth and the brandy he had made her swallow had made her sleepy; she had no idea how long it had taken to drive back but she roused herself as he stopped before the house and when he opened her door she got out, to be held firmly and urged into the house. The hall seemed full of people but it was Alicia she went to. The child had been crying and ran to her at once and Beatrice knelt down and caught her in a tight hug.

'Where were you?' wailed Alicia. 'Papa looked everywhere for you. I thought you'd run away...'

'My darling, why should I run away when I am so happy here living with you all? I had an adventure, quite an exciting one, I'll tell you all about it presently, but first I must go and get out of this coat and do something about my hair.'

Alicia flung her arms around her neck. 'I'll come with you and help you. Papa can come too.'

Beatrice looked up then. Gijs was standing by the door, watching them. There was a look on his face she hadn't seen before and she scrambled to her feet although she wasn't sure what she was going to do. Whatever it was wasn't going to be done, though. He said evenly, 'We have all been worried. Do go with Mrs Bilder, my dear, and change your things.'

She stood still and glanced around her. The Bilders and both the maids were there and she smiled apologetically at them and Gijs said, 'I came home early, intending to go with you for a run and brought Mies with me—and we have an unexpected visitor...'

Beatrice turned her head and smiled uncertainly at Mies and then opened her mouth to speak and closed it again. Tom was standing there.

'Surprised?' He smiled widely. 'I thought I'd take a look at Leiden and look you up at the same time. I met your husband at the hospital and he kindly invited me. I must say you have a delightful home, Beatrice.'

It was Alicia who spoke. 'I don't like him,' she said loudly. 'Why does he call you Beatrice?'

Beatrice still hadn't spoken. Gijs broke the silence, saying easily, 'Beatrice needs to get out of those damp clothes. Alicia, go with her and give her a hand.' He crossed the hall and took Beatrice's hands in his.

'Don't hurry, my dear. I'll get Mrs Bilder to send up some tea for you—you're tired and shocked, you will feel better presently. If Mies and—er—Tom care to they might like to dine with us and then you can tell us exactly what happened.'

Beatrice looked up into his face. There was nothing there to show her what he was really thinking. On an impulse she leaned up and kissed him and then went up the staircase with Alicia clinging to one hand.

CHAPTER NINE

WHEN Beatrice went downstairs again presently, Alicia with her, she looked the picture of serenity. She had changed into a cream satin blouse and a brown velvet skirt, swathed her abundant hair in a french pleat and applied a careful make-up. While she had dressed she had had time to get over the surprise of seeing Tom. He had a nerve, she considered, coming to visit them so soon after their wedding, and uninvited. Perhaps he hadn't believed that they were really getting married . . .

She went into the drawing-room with Alicia hanging onto an arm and Gijs crossed the room to them. 'You're all right? Warm and dry again? Good. Come and sit by the fire and tell us about it.'

There was no sign of the anger which had been in his face when he had reached her car; he looked kind and concerned—just exactly as a loving husband should look in the circumstances, she reflected wryly.

She told them about her afternoon then, making it a light-hearted account. Mies and Tom had laughed a good deal and she was surprised to see how well they appeared to get on together. Tom was being charming and it seemed as though Mies found him a delightful companion. She glanced at Gijs once or twice and saw that he was watching them casually while they all talked. Presently Alicia went to bed and they had drinks before she and Gijs went to say goodnight to Alicia.

Going up the staircase side by side with Gijs, Beatrice said, 'They seem to get on awfully well together!' She paused to look at him. 'I wouldn't want Mies to get taken in...'

'My dear girl, Mies is a tough little lady. If any one is taken in it will be your Tom.'

'He is not my Tom,' snapped Beatrice in a sudden temper. 'No more than Mies is your Mies.'

Gijs didn't reply, only smiled a little, a smile which she didn't see.

When they joined the others they were planning to meet the following day. 'Mies is going to show me round Leiden,' said Tom smugly. 'A pity I can only stay for such a short time.'

'Well, I shall come to London and you shall show me round there,' said Mies. She meant it too, decided Beatrice.

She felt a thrill of pride as they went into the dining-room; it was splendid with silver and porcelain on a linen and lace cloth and the bowl of early spring flowers she had arranged that morning. She enjoyed her visits to the kitchen and Mevrouw Bilder, discussing the menus with Bilder patiently translating, and the dinner they had planned was well chosen—tomato and orange soup, Dover sole, devilled new potatoes, courgettes cooked in red wine and boiled celery with a béchamel sauce, and these followed by Russian raspberry pudding, served piping hot. The conversation, skilfully guided by the professor, was light and amusing. They lingered over their cheese and biscuits and presently went back to drink their coffee by the fire in the drawing-room. Fred, nicely full of his own dinner, took up his usual place by his master, looking sleepy but peeping every now and then at Tom. His little yellow eyes could look quite malevolent; it was as though he knew that Tom wasn't a welcome guest...

It was really most extraordinary, thought Beatrice, bidding the pair of them goodbye. Mies had asked Tom to drive her back and e had agreed with an eagerness she hadn't xpected of him. She stood in the hall beside Gijs, watching Bilder close the door as the ound of Tom's hired car died away, and then ent back to the drawing-room.

She sat down again although it was quite ate and picked up her knitting because she as aware of a wave of ill-temper washing ver her.

'Why did you ask Tom to stay?' she deanded in a voice which to her ears sounded ery like that of a nagging wife.

The professor had sat down in his chair too; e looked the picture of content and satisaction. 'One could hardly send the fellow out a that shocking weather,' he observed mildly. Besides, he and Mies took an instant liking o each other.'

Beatrice knitted half a row of purl and lain. 'How could you do that? Mies is a— n old friend of yours and you let her be harmed by that man. She's far too nice.' She rowned; nice wasn't the right word but she ouldn't think of another.

'Mies is attractive and a pleasant comanion; everyone likes her because she sees to that they do. She is also a lady who can ok after herself, someone who, when she arries, will be the dominating partner. As I

have said, if I guess correctly, they will each
have what they want. Your Tom will have the
means to climb the ladder to a fashionable
practice——' the professor made no effort to
disguise the contempt in his voice '—and Mies
will have a husband she can dominate.'

'You mean that they would marry just for
those reasons? But that's so wrong.' She
stopped and bit her lip; she and Gijs had
married for reasons too, good reasons, all of
them; he had said that Mies and Tom were
attracted to each other. She supposed that if
they liked—loved—each other they would
accept each other's motives.

She remembered something. 'He's not my
Tom,' she snapped, 'I said so...'

The professor watched her from under
heavy lids. 'A slip of the tongue,' he said
blandly.

She wondered during the next few days if
she would see anything more of Tom but there
was no sign of him, only towards the end of
the week Mies came one morning just as
Beatrice was bidding Juffrouw Blank
goodbye in halting Dutch. The ladies wished
each other good morning and Mies followed
Beatrice into the sitting-room at the back of
the house—a room Beatrice had made her
own.

'You don't mind me coming like this? You are not going out or having visitors?'

'I'm just going to have coffee—have some with me?' invited Beatrice. 'And I'm not going out, not yet. The *dominee*'s wife is coming to tea this afternoon and bringing some of the ladies from the village—something to do with flowers for the church. I'm rather dreading it.'

'No need.' Mies had settled herself in a chair by the cheerful fire and tossed her coat over a table. 'I will tell you what you must do. They will ask you to join their circle and you will be expected to send flowers to the church when it is your turn. Of course, because Gijs is by far the richest and most important person living here, you will be expected to send the most expensive flowers. If you give money for charity that is also a good idea. You have been to the church?'

Beatrice sat down in the small rosewood *bergère* with its delicate, faded upholstery. 'Yes, I've seen it. I like the *dominee*, and his wife speaks English.'

'Then you will enjoy your afternoon.'

Bilder brought in the coffee and Beatrice poured it and handed the plate of wafer-thin biscuits. 'Will you stay for lunch, Mies?'

'I am having lunch with Tom. He return
this afternoon,' Mies smiled widely, 'and i
a few days' time I go to London so that w
may see more of each other.' She glanced a
Beatrice. 'You do not mind?'

'Me? Mind? Why should I? I—that i
Tom...'

'You do not need to explain,' said Mie
comfortably. 'He is a philanderer, is he not
Which does not worry me at all. I shall hol
the purse strings and he will not stray far; h
is too ambitious for that. We shall be happ
together.' She took another biscuit an
munched it. 'We met here—you know that—
and I knew at once that he would suit me ver
well and he felt the same. We shall marry.'

'But you have only just met...'

'You and Gijs—did you not only ju
meet?' asked Mies. 'And did you not kno
at once that you wished to marry?' Sh
smiled. 'Perhaps not you, Beatrice, but I hav
known Gijs for many years; he makes up h
mind at once and that is that.'

'Yes, well...' said Beatrice inadequately. '
do hope that you and Tom will be happy.'

'You are doubtful because you know hi
quite well, do you not? But do not worry,
see his faults—he is selfish and I think a litt
greedy and conceited, but these things do n

worry me. He needs a wife who will—how do you say?—boss him, and that I shall do. Now Gijs is not like that but you will know that. He said to me, "Mies, I need a wife and a mother for Alicia, and I know exactly the kind of woman to be both".' She smiled. 'You, Beatrice.'

Beatrice managed a smile. 'Tell me about his first wife—such a pretty name.'

'Such a pretty woman too, but not good or kind. I think that she never loved Gijs and if he ever loved her his love died very soon. She left him with Alicia, you know, and went away with another man and died soon after that. It is good that he has you, now he can have a home again and Alicia is very fond of you.'

'I'm fond of her, she's a darling little girl. How are you going to England?'

'From Schiphol; it's so quick. I am to stay in London and Tom will spend his free time with me. We have much to discuss—many plans...'

Mies looked thoughtfully at Beatrice. 'You are not quite happy about us, I think. I am not you, I am tough and I know what I want and I intend to have it. Tom is right for me; he will be a success because I have the money to make that so and I will wear the trousers.'

They both laughed then and presently Mies
went away and Beatrice took the patient Fred
for his walk. She went a long way, thinking
hard. Tom was out of the way, so was Mies;
that left the way clear for her and Gijs to get
to know each other, for him to fall in love,
perhaps. She went home pondering ways and
means.

The ladies from the village duly arrived,
explained in a mixture of both languages
about the flowers and what they expected of
Beatrice, drank tea from little porcelain cups
and ate the dainty little biscuits Mevrouw
Bilder had made and presently went home,
leaving Beatrice to go to her room and decide
what she would wear that evening—something to catch Gijs's eye... Bilder had gone
to fetch Alicia and, while she was still pondering the merits of the satin blouse and the
velvet skirt again or a less eye-catching but
very pretty blue jersey dress she hadn't yet
worn, the little girl came tearing upstairs with
Fred at her side.

She flung herself at Beatrice, full of her day
at school, and Beatrice sat down on the side
of the bed to listen.

'I am hungry,' declared Alicia, rolling her
eyes dramatically.

'Well, you shall have your tea, little one, but first I must get dressed.'

'You look nice like that with not much clothing,' Alicia told her. She picked up the blue dress, 'And you must wear this. Papa will like you in this.'

Beatrice hoped that he would and got into it without more ado. It was indeed pretty; well pleased with her appearance, she went to the playroom with Alicia and sat down and had a cup of tea with Nanny while Alicia had her own tea.

Nanny eyed her. 'The master likes blue,' she said, and nodded.

They went downstairs presently, she and Alicia and Fred, and into the drawing-room where Alicia sprawled on the floor with a jigsaw puzzle, Fred spread himself before the fire and Beatrice arranged herself in her usual chair with the small rose-coloured lampshade shedding a flattering light over her person. She had her knitting and she was aware that she presented a pleasing picture to anyone coming into the room.

Someone did come in very shortly, but it wasn't Gijs. It was Bilder to say that there was a telephone call for *mevrouw* if she would be good enough to take it. He plugged the instrument in and handed it to her and went away again.

Probably her mother or Gijs' parents, thought Beatrice and said, 'hello.'

It was Gijs and he spoke abruptly and without preamble. 'I shall be late home, Beatrice. Don't wait for dinner or stay up for me. Ask Bilder to lock up if I'm not back by eleven o'clock.'

'Well, yes, all right,' said Beatrice. 'Is something the matter? You're all right?' and when he didn't answer she said, 'Gijs...?'

She was aware of other sounds, voices, the clink of glasses, someone shouting, and then a woman's voice calling urgently. She said, 'Gijs?' again but he had hung up.

She put the phone down with a shaking hand, astonished at the strong feelings she felt, but when Alicia asked her anxiously if it had been Papa and if he was coming home, she explained in her matter-of-fact way and went in search of Bilder. He heard her out and nodded sympathetically. 'The professor works too hard, *mevrouw*. I will serve dinner at the usual hour?'

'Yes, please.' She smiled at him and went back to spend another half an hour with Alicia and, when the child had gone to bed, sat down to her solitary meal. She had

planned it carefully that morning with
Mevrouw Bilder. The table looked charming
with the flowers at its centre and candles in
the silver candelabrum. They had decided on
chicken *á la* king because Gijs liked it. The
food tasted like sawdust in her mouth; she ate
some of it and, not wishing to disappoint
Mevrouw Bilder, did her best with the pastry
basket filled with fruit which followed the
lemon sorbet, and all the time she wondered
about Gijs. There had been no doubt in her
mind that it had been a party of some sort
but why hadn't Gijs said so? And he had
sounded remote, as though he hadn't wanted
to spare the time to phone her.

She went back to the fire, allowing her
imagination full rein until it was time to let
Fred out for his final run and take him along
to the kitchen for the night. She stayed for a
few minutes talking to the Bilders and the two
maids and then took herself off to bed, daw-
dling over her undressing so that it was almost
midnight before she got into bed at last. The
house was quiet, Bilder had long since se-
cured the doors and windows and gone to his
own bed and she lay awake, the curtains in
her room pulled back so that she would see
the car's lights coming through the village and
into the grounds. She willed them to appear,

but nothing happened. Presently she went to sleep.

She woke to see the car's lights disappear round the side of the house to the garages and sat up in bed to turn on the bedside lamp. It was half-past four in the morning. At that hour of the morning thoughts were not always conducive to common sense. Beatrice scrambled out of bed, dragged on her dressing-gown, thrust her feet into slippers and went silently down the staircase. She was on the bottom step when Gijs let himself into the house.

The sight of him, looking as unconcerned as though it were the afternoon and not the small hours, stirred her to rage. 'About time too,' she told him in a vibrant whisper, 'I can't think why you bother to come home at this hour. You might just as well have made a night of it.'

He had stopped by the door, now he put his bag down, threw his coat on top of it and leaned against the door frame. He didn't say anything and she couldn't see him very clearly in the dim light of the lamp on the side table. 'You were at a party,' said Beatrice, casting discretion to the winds and giving her imagination full rein, 'I could hear the glasses and people talking and a woman . . .' She stopped to gain her breath. 'It was a party, wasn't it?'

The professor sighed gently, 'Indeed it was.'

'You should be ashamed of yourself,' said Beatrice, still in a whisper although she longed to shout and throw something at him. Indeed, her glance dwelt on a particularly ugly and priceless Sèvres vase on the side table, a look which he rightly interpreted.

'No, no, Beatrice—it is hideous, I agree, but we don't want to disturb the household, do we?'

He walked towards her, smiling, and she could see now that his face was drawn and very tired. 'You'd better get to bed,' she said coldly, 'for what's left of the night.'

She started up the staircase. Halfway she stopped. 'Do you want a hot drink? I told Bilder to leave coffee on the Aga.'

'No.' He spoke in a silky voice she hadn't heard before. 'What I do want is to shake you until your teeth rattle and then wring your lovely neck.'

He turned on his heel and went into his study and after a few moments she went back to her room to climb into her cold bed and think about what he had said. 'He must hate me,' she muttered, and burst into tears. 'Well,

I hate him too,' she declared. She said it twice since she needed to be convinced.

She went down to breakfast a few hours later, glad of Alicia's company, and found that he had already left the house. She tried not to notice Bilder's slightly reproachful look, crumbled toast while Alicia had her breakfast and then got out the car and drove her to school. She was driving back through the town when she saw Mies waving at her from the pavement and pulled in to the kerb.

Mies poked her head through the window. 'My dear, what a night! Gijs must be worn out. I hope you put him to bed and told him to have a good sleep...'

'He went to the hospital as usual,' said Beatrice. 'He had left the house before Alicia and I got down to breakfast.'

'He's mad,' said Mies and opened the door and got in beside Beatrice. 'I dare say he didn't tell you anything...' She glanced at Beatrice.

'He telephoned...'

'He found time for that? It was just fate that he should be driving past the Doelen restaurant when some waiter or other went screaming into the street, calling for help. I dare say Gijs didn't tell you the half of it, but he went to see what was the matter and found these two men with severed arteries and I don't know what else—there'd been a party and they were all drunk, you can imagine what it was like to try and get any of them to help... He went to the hospital with them and stayed to give a hand...'

'But Gijs is a haematologist,' said Beatrice.

Mies gave her a questioning look. 'He's a first-rate surgeon too. You didn't know any of this, did you?'

Beatrice shook her head. 'No. Oh, Mies, I thought he was at a party and when he came home I was very angry.'

Mies started to say something and then changed her mind. 'Well, you can explain all that to him when he comes home this evening,' she said comfortingly. 'I must go now—I'm meeting some friends.' She got out of the car and Beatrice drove back to Aaledijk, to spend the rest of the day trying out a variety of speeches with which to greet Gijs when he came home.

That afternoon she fetched Alicia from school and after tea with her and Nanny went to her room with Alicia and Fred and changed into the blue dress. No knitting this time; she had bought some embroidery to do, a complicated pattern which needed stitches counted and dozens of different-coloured silks, but it made a nice change from the knitting and she hoped that the sight of her, sitting by the fire, plying her needle might help to ease matters...

It was shortly after six o'clock when she heard the car turn in at the gates and her heart began to thump and then to drop into her shoes as Alicia said, 'That's Papa—there is another car too.'

She darted from the room, Fred with her, and Beatrice perforce had to abandon her carefully planned pose in the softly lighted room and follow her. There were voices in the hall. When she reached it, Alicia was hugging her father, Fred was loping to and fro in a pleased way and there were two people with Gijs. She knew one of them; the director of the hospital—Professor ter Vosse—and presumably the cosily built elderly lady with him was his wife.

She went to meet them, flashing a smile at Gijs at the same time, shook hands with the professor, exchanged greetings with his wife, and urged them to take off their coats and come into the drawing room.

Bilder, appearing silently, took coats and scarves, exchanged a few murmured words with his master and went away again. Beatrice, exchanging small talk with her guests, cast a swift glance at Gijs. He looked perfectly at ease and when he spoke to her she could find no fault in his manner; only his eyes, as they rested on her, were cold.

'We must not stay,' declared the director. 'We are on our way to dine with friends at Woerden, but we could not resist the chance to see you again, Beatrice.'

They sat chatting for half an hour, drinking the coffee Bilder had brought, and presently got up to go. 'Such a pity,' remarked Professor ter Vosse as Bilder helped him into his coat, 'that Gijs must go away at such short notice.' He smiled kindly at Beatrice. 'But of course as a doctor's wife you will be prepared to accept that and of course it is not possible for you to accompany him with this little one at home.' He patted Alicia on the head and beamed around him.

'Well, of course not,' agreed Beatrice. 'We wouldn't dream of it ...'

Mevrouw ter Vosse tapped her arm. 'Never mind, my dear, when Gijs is director you will have him to yourself as I have my dear Bernard.'

They shook hands and kissed and Professor ter Vosse said as he went, 'I am so glad that you persuaded us to come with you, Gijs— you must both dine with us soon ...'

So Gijs had invited them deliberately, reflected Beatrice, and what was all that talk of going away? There was no chance to ask then; Alicia was still with them, plying her father with questions, telling him about her lessons. Nanny came for her presently and, alone with Gijs at last, Beatrice took a deep breath. 'You're going away?'

Gijs had picked up the handful of post on the table by his chair and was leafing through it. 'To Northern Ireland.' He spoke casually and looked at her briefly.

'But that's...' She was going to say 'dangerous' and thought better of it. 'When do you have to go?'

'This evening.' He took his pocket watch from his waistcoat and looked at it. 'In about half an hour.'

'But you can't...' began Beatrice and was stopped by his raised eyebrows.

'Can't?' he asked coldly. He put his letters down, bent to pat Fred and got to his feet.

'You could have told me—I wanted to talk to you, to explain...'

'I think that perhaps we should wait until we have the leisure for that, don't you, Beatrice?'

She had got up too. 'Gijs, I'm sorry—I didn't know...'

'It isn't just that, my dear. You didn't—
ou don't trust me. We have been married for
uch a short time and you are ready to believe
iny nonsense that comes into your head.'

He wasn't angry, she realised, or if he was
ie was concealing it very well. 'It's not what
ou think,' she began.

'Had we better not go and say goodnight
o Alicia?'

They went upstairs together. 'You will tele-
ihone?' asked Beatrice.

'If that is possible.'

She listened while he explained in his calm
oice that he would be away for a few days
ir perhaps a week. 'But you will have
Beatrice, *liefje*, so you won't be lonely. Take
ood care of each other and look after Fred
or me.'

He went away to his room and Beatrice
vent back to the drawing-room to sit with
Fred until presently Gijs came in.

She got up and went towards him. 'You will
ake care?'

He didn't answer that. 'Bilder will look
ifter you both and my father knows that I
hall be away; he'll drive over to see you.'

'We'll be all right. I'll take care of Alicia.'

They were standing very close, for a
ioment she thought that he would kiss her

but he didn't. His '*tot ziens*' sounded almost
casual as he went into the hall where Bilder
was waiting to open the door. She followed
him and stood listening to the quiet hum of
the Bentley as it went through the gates and
into the village.

For the second time in the last few days she
sat down to her solitary dinner, aware that
Bilder was eyeing her in a fatherly fashion so
that to eat some of it was imperative. As he
took away her plate she said, 'While the professor is away, Bilder, there's no need to serve
my meals here. I could have them in the
sitting-room or on a tray.'

'Of course, *mevrouw*, just as you wish. It
is to be hoped that the professor will return
very soon.'

Beatrice agreed with mixed feelings; she
longed to see Gijs again but she still had a lot
of explaining to do.

She went to the drawing-room presently
with Fred for company; a few rows of knitting
might calm her down and presently she began
to review the next few days. She would telephone her mother and father and tell them
how happy she was, she would present a
smiling face to her father-in-law if he came to
see her, and she must remember that she had
accepted an invitation to drink coffee with the

ominee's wife and a select circle of ladies
rom the village. Then there was the hospital
all in just over a week's time. They had ac-
epted that invitation too and she cheered up
t the thought for Gijs would have to be back
or it. It was a rather grand affair, he had told
er, at the same time suggesting that she might
ike to get a new dress.

'I will too,' said Beatrice, addressing Fred.
I'll take Alicia to school tomorrow and go
n to den Haag. I'll buy something really
orgeous.'

A practical girl, she studied the map of the
ity before she went to bed and with a little
dvice from Bilder had no difficulty in
arking the car and finding her way to the
hopping centre. The boutiques were tucked
way down arcades or narrow lanes and she
earched each of them in turn until she finally
ound exactly what she was looking for. Blue
hiffon, because Alicia had told her that Gijs
ked blue, a lovely floating dress, deceptively
imple while at the same time making the most
f her splendid figure. It cost a lot but she
ad money of her own as well as a bank ac-
ount Gijs had now arranged for her.
'ortified by a cup of coffee, she bought gold
id sandals—mere straps and high heels—and
ent back to the car. On the way home she

stopped before she reached Leiden and had
more coffee and a ham roll. When she got
home it was to hear from Bilder that the professor had telephoned to ask if all was well.
He would telephone again when possible, said
Bilder.

His father came the next day and stayed to
lunch. Beatrice liked him and they got on well
together. She and Alicia were to go to den
Haag at the weekend if Gijs wasn't back
'Can't have you feeling lonely,' he told her
breezily. 'Such a pity Gijs had to go away so
soon after your marriage.'

Beatrice replied suitably and added, 'But
perhaps Gijs will be home by then.'

'I think not, but if he is then you must come
at some other time. We wish very much to get
to know you, my dear.'

She rang her mother that evening and told
her about the new dress and the ball and when
that lady started asking questions she said
cheerfully, 'Here's Alicia, longing to talk to
you.'

Despite the prospect of the ball and the new
gown, coffee with the village ladies and
lessons with her stern teacher, the days were
long and each night when she went to bed she
allowed herself the luxury of a good cry. The
weekend, spent with her in-laws and lapped

around with kindness, came and went and in another two days the ball would take place. Gijs had rung twice, brief calls to ask if everything was all right. He said nothing about coming home and she hadn't asked although she had longed to know, but she did remind him about the ball.

'I shall be home before then,' he had told her, his voice pleasant and quite impersonal.

The evening before the ball she went to bed convinced that he wasn't coming, but when she and Alicia went down to breakfast in the morning he was there, sitting at the table, looking for all the world as though he had never been away. Alicia rushed at him, demanding to know when he had come home. I didn't hear Fred—he didn't bark...'

'Well, *liefje*, it was very early this morning and besides he knew that it was I so that he had no need to bark.' He looked across at Beatrice. 'I didn't disturb you?'

'No, you must have been very quiet. You had a successful trip?'

'I believe so. And what have you been doing with yourselves?'

It was Alicia who answered, filling the awkward silences with chatter, and presently he got up from the table.

'You're not going to the hospital?' Beatrice's voice was sharp.

'A few small matters to clear up. The ball starts at nine o'clock, doesn't it? We don't need to be there for half an hour after that—I'll be back in good time to change.'

He kissed his small daughter, bent to peck Beatrice on a cheek and went away with Fred at his heels.

Beatrice took Alicia to school, walked miles with Fred, conferred with Mevrouw Bilder about a suitable light meal should it be needed that evening, did the homework Juffrouw Blanke insisted upon her doing each day, ate a lunch she didn't want and, after another brisk walk with Fred, took herself off to her room where she examined her face for spots and wrinkles, did her nails and got out the new dress. That filled in the time nicely until she could go downstairs again and have tea. There was no sign of Gijs; she supposed that he would be home later. Bilder had fetched Alicia and she went upstairs presently to talk to Nanny and play spillikins with Alicia until bedtime. It was almost eight o'clock by now and time for her to dress. She lay in the bath for a long time, rehearsing just what she was going to say to Gijs. There would surely be time before they left for the ball. She dressed

owly and presently went down the stairs in
:r lovely dress, treading carefully because of
:r high heels. There was no sign of Gijs and
ie house was very quiet. She had gone to kiss
licia goodnight and display the dress and
iere was nothing for it but to put her velvet
)at on one of the chairs in the hall and sit
. the drawing-room.

It was after half-past eight when he came
)me. He came into the room unhurriedly. 'I
on't keep you long,' he told her. 'Is Alicia
:leep?'

'No—at least she wasn't ten minutes ago.
he wanted to say goodnight to you.'

'I'll go there first.' He spoke pleasantly—
: could have been addressing a chance
:quaintance.

The long-case clock in the hall chimed nine
'clock, echoed by the delicate chimes of the
racket clock in the drawing room and it was
n minutes after that before Gijs came into
ie room. The sight of him, resplendent in
hite tie and tails, almost took her breath but
l she said was, 'Have we time to talk?'

'Hardly. If we leave now we should arrive
the right time, I think.'

There was no point in arguing; she went
to the hall with him and he helped her on
ith the coat as Bilder went to open the door.

'Don't wait up,' said the professor as the left the house. 'I dare say we shall be ve late.'

Bilder inclined his head gravely. 'A pleasa evening, *mevrouw*—Professor.'

Beatrice spent the short journey trying think of something to say but it wasn't a good, her head was empty, and only the speeches she had so carefully thought o rolled back and forth in her head. She wo dered if she would be too tired to make o of them when they got back home. They wer she considered, well thought out and sensib and she would utter them in a reasonable voi so that he would see that she meant ever word.

The ball was well under way. She went aw; to leave her coat and make sure that her ha was still immaculate and then she joined hi in the vast entrance hall of the universit There were a great many people millir around and even more dancing in th ballroom beyond. They greeted the direct and his wife and Gijs swung her on to th dance floor. She was a good dancer and s was he. Just for a little while she forgot th muddle she had made of things and gav herself up to the delight of being in his arm She could have danced forever but the bar stopped too soon and they were surrounded by his friends and colleagues and she was swept away once more to dance with an unending stream of partners. It wasn't until the supper dance that Gijs sought her out, guiding her smoothly round the room, carrying on a trivial conversation. In the supper room they sat with half a dozen other people and when they had finished she was whisked away by the director to dance a very correct foxtrot while he told her what a splendid man she had married . . .

From time to time she glimpsed Gijs, smiling brightly at him as she floated past with a succession of partners, but it wasn't until the band began the slow sweet strains of the last waltz that he whisked her away on to the floor. Taking care not to look above his white tie, she recognised this as her chance. There might not be another one; it would be the small hours before they were home and for all she knew he might have left the house by the time she got down to breakfast in the morning. She took a deep breath and discovered that she had forgotten every word of her well rehearsed speech. She glanced up at her husband, who gave her a bland look which didn't deceive her in the least. Somewhere under that calm face he was amused. She said softly, 'You'd better listen to what I want to say—you haven't given me a chance. Why didn't you tell me it wasn't a party? Why...?'

'My dear, I did tell you; you wanted to throw a vase at me.'

'Don't you dare laugh; it's what any wife would have done.'

His arm tightened around her. 'Why were you angry, Beatrice?'

She smiled sweetly at a passing couple. 'Of course I was angry; I thought—oh, never mind that now, it's all such a muddle and so awkward. I was jealous—I didn't know that I could be but I was. I've—I've fallen in love with you, Gijs, and I wasn't meant to, was I? We were to be good friends and we were but I don't think that's possible any more.' She paused for breath. She twisted the poesy ring on her finger. '"You and no other".'

'We met at a dance,' said the professor, and something in his voice made her look at him. 'I fell in love with you then and there! I have been waiting for you to fall in love with me. It seems that our fates are to be resolved on the dance-floor.'

He whirled her through an archway leading to a big conservatory behind the ballroom, wrapped her in a rib-crushing embrace and kissed her hard.

'I've been wanting to do that for a very long time,' he told her, and he did it again. 'I love you and no other, my darling.'

Beatrice kissed him back. 'Oh, Gijs, what shall we do now?'

He smiled down at her happy face. 'My dearest love, shall we go home?'

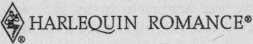

HARLEQUIN ROMANCE®

brings you

The written word has played an important role in all our romances in our Sealed With a Kiss series so far and next month's #3378 *Angels Do Have Wings* by Helen Brooks is no exception.

But just as Angel Murray was writing a long letter to her best friend explaining that nothing exciting ever happened to her—something did. A rich, tall and utterly gorgeous stranger walked into her life and casually turned it upside down.

What could a man like Hunter Ryan possibly want with a girl like her? Despite the attraction that flared between them, they were worlds apart. Angel could never reconcile herself to a temporary affair and that was clearly all he was offering her. But Hunter's charm was proving all too persuasive. And as for his kiss…

From the celebrated author of
And the Bride Wore Black.

SWAK-7

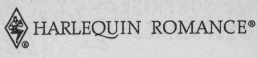

PRIZE SURPRISE SWEEPSTAKES!

This month's prize:

BEAUTIFUL WEDGWOOD CHINA!

This month, as a special surprise, we're giving away a bone china dinner service for eight by Wedgwood**, one of England's most prestigious manufacturers!

Think how beautiful your table will look, set with lovely Wedgwood china in the casual Countryware pattern! Each five-piece place setting includes dinner plate, salad plate, soup bowl and cup and saucer.

The facing page contains two Entry Coupons (as does every book you received this shipment). Complete and return *all* the entry coupons; **the more times you enter, the better your chances of winning!**

Then keep your fingers crossed, because you'll find out by September 15, 1995 if you're the winner!

Remember: The more times you enter, the better your chances of winning!*

PRIZE SURPRISE
SWEEPSTAKES
OFFICIAL ENTRY COUPON

This entry must be received by: AUGUST 30, 1995
This month's winner will be notified by: SEPTEMBER 15, 1995

YES, I want to win the Wedgwood china service for eight! Please enter me in the drawing and let me know if I've won!

Name_____

Address _____ Apt. _____

City   State/Prov.   Zip/Postal Code

Account #_____

Return entry with invoice in reply envelope.

© 1995 HARLEQUIN ENTERPRISES LTD.   CWW KAL

PRIZE SURPRISE
SWEEPSTAKES
OFFICIAL ENTRY COUPON

This entry must be received by: AUGUST 30, 1995
This month's winner will be notified by: SEPTEMBER 15, 1995

YES, I want to win the Wedgwood china service for eight! Please enter me in the drawing and let me know if I've won!

Name_____

Address _____ Apt. _____

City   State/Prov.   Zip/Postal Code

Account #_____

Return entry with invoice in reply envelope.

© 1995 HARLEQUIN ENTERPRISES LTD.   CWW KAL